THE TERROR OUT OF SPACE

By
DWIGHT V. SWAIN

ARMCHAIR FICTION & MUSIC
PO Box 4369, Medford, Oregon 97504

*For more information about Armchair Books and products, visit our
website at...*

www.armchairfiction.com

Or email us at...

armchairfiction@yahoo.com

TRAPPED ON A TERRIFYING ALIEN WORLD

Fred Boone found himself in a no win situation. He was being hunted by agents of a powerful interplanetary cartel; even worse, the woman he loved had spurned him; and now he found himself trapped on a distant world surrounded by an alien intelligence—an intelligence so formidable that it could take the most horrifying creatures and the most terrifying situations from one's worst nightmares and change them into reality.

This thrilling and sometimes chilling science fiction adventure tale is a perfect example of why Dwight V. Swain was one of the master storytellers from the golden age of science fiction.

FOR A COMPLETE SECOND NOVEL, TURN TO PAGE 89

CAST OF CHARACTERS

FRED BOONE

A tough outer space veteran, his big problem was being hated and hunted by one of the most powerful men in the galaxy.

EILEEN REY

She was a seasoned extraterrestrial biologist who looked at Boone as an interloper and a threat to her career.

MARTIN KROBIS

He lusted for power, and he hatched an incredible scheme to make himself more powerful than the Federation itself.

LOR

Born on a distant moon, he was the son of two humans, yet he possessed unbelievable alien powers.

TERREL

His independent space consortium was the only thing that stood between Martin Krobis and his plan to dominate the solar system.

SCHILLING

This space lawyer possessed a keen legal mind. But he was hired to defend Boone against seemingly impossible odds.

THE HELGAE

Were they merely harmless alien blobs, or were they intelligent beings responsible for space attacks by alien monstrosities?

CHAPTER ONE

IT WAS a good proposition, the way the lean, gray man from Associated Independents told it. He ticked off the points on his fingers:

"Ten thousand credits an Earth year, Boone, win or lose. Full command of the field force. Five per cent cut on the profits if you get a mekronal processing unit in production on one of the unassigned satellites ahead of the Cartel."

"Sorry Terral." Again, Boone glanced at his chronox. "It's like I said. Any other time I might be interested. But right now I've got something else on my mind."

"Fifteen thousand, then. And ten per cent if you spot in more than one satellite." Terral leaned forward. "Hell, man, that's more than you can hope to make as a GX if you stay with the Cartel!"

Boone grinned, after a fashion. "Sorry."

The lean man pushed back abruptly and gulped down his drink. "Then it is the woman!" he accused. A spark of pale fire lighted behind the gray eyes. Even in the dimness of the thil-shop, Boone couldn't miss the tension. "Krobis shoves her in ahead of you, but you'd still throw away your future—"

Boone brought his own glass down on the tanach table top, just hard enough so that it clicked a curt, sharp period to the other's sentence. "And what makes that your business?"

For the moment Terral's narrow jaws seemed to widen at the hinges. His lips peeled back, as if he were about to say something raw and cutting. Then, reconsidering, he breathed in deep instead and slumped loose in his seat. The thin lips drew together in a crooked smile. "My business—? Nothing, Boone. Nothing at all."

"That's the way I see it, too." Boone got up. "Good night, Terral."

He strode on out, not bothering to shake hands or look back.

The night closed in upon him—the night, and the narrow street; the alien sounds and smells and stir of Gandor City. A cadet from the Federation fleet pushed past him, a moss-furred Callistan crustach perched up on his shoulder. Behind the cadet

came two spask-masked berlon prospectors, up from the Hertzog fields, leading their lumbering flipper-tentacled coddob by a chain run through its gill-slits. The throb of the atmosphere compressors pressed in like a giant heartbeat, punctuated by the rattle of surface carriers, the shrill wail of tricol pipes. A sweetish, slightly nauseous scent of theswood flares and Martian paggod eddied from the doorway of a greasy-looking grill that placarded "Genuine Earth Meats—No Synthetics. No Alien Substitutes!"

Once more, Boone checked his chronox.

Somewhere in the void was a planet with a new element that could transform men into supermen. It was Boone's job to find that world—if he survived—

The Terror Out Of Space

By

Dwight V. Swain

It was less than an hour till the end of the cycle now.

In spite of himself, Boone's belly tightened. Turning at the first intersection, he headed for the carrier station.

The IC flight was already on the line and waiting. He found a seat next to a dour-faced tech whose eye-whites showed green with mekronal infusion.

THE carrier wheeled slowly forward into the lock that sealed off Gandor City's precious, bubble-pressured air supply from the bleak world outside. A moment later the lock's outer hatch opened. Climbing on its anti-gravitational beam—slowly, at first; then faster and faster—the carrier lanced out across the star-spangled black velvet of the Ganymedan sky.

The minutes dragged. Crags and peaks came and went below; then the dull gray wash of a cliff-bound sea of liquid gas. Off to the left, the sky took on a scarlet-purple tint, reflection of Jupiter's great Red Spot.

Down again, then. Down through another hatch, into another lock.

Its inner seal opened. The carrier swept into the bubble proper, settling onto the clean-swept ramp with its glaring forspark lights and the sign that said:

INTERPLANETARY CARTELS
UNLIMITED
MEKRONAL PROCESSING
DIVISION
GANYMEDAN ADVANCE BASE

Boone passed through the scanner unit; bared his ID plate for the guard.

"Back early, aren't you, Mister Boone?" The guard grinned. "Guess it makes a difference when you go alone. Though I will say that new job's a nice break for Miss Rey."

Boone nodded, not speaking.

"She goes out tonight, doesn't she?" The guard's face grew

sober. "Hope she makes it okay. That Titan run is no picnic—not with this monster business hitting half the ships. Bucking that kind of thing ain't my idea of a woman's job, no matter how high it rates nor how much it pays."

"She'll make it, all right."

"Sure." The guard's eyes shifted away from Boone's. "Sure, Mister Boone. She'll make it."

Boone passed on.

Inside the personnel compound, he looked at his chronox again.

Only half an hour now till Eileen was scheduled to grav-off.

Barely time for the job he had to do...

Turning in at his own quarters, he strode down the empty, echoing corridor to his room; closed the door behind him.

The nerve-gun lay in the top drawer, as always—sleek, grim, coldly lethal. Stiff-fingered, Boone checked the charge, then slid the weapon beneath his blouse and turned to go.

But Eileen's picture on the corner stand caught him...held him.

Her picture, and the memories that went with it.

He picked it up; stared at it.

She was wearing her first uniform, with its student stripes, the silver comet Cartel insignia shining against the dark blue of the lapels. But even official tailoring and close-combed regulation hairdo couldn't hide her radiance. The blue eyes laughed with sheer love of living. Her lips showed soft and smiling, better styled for kisses than commands.

That was the Eileen Rey whom he remembered...the Eileen of his own student unit days, the girl who'd climbed rank after rank beside him through Interplanetary Cartels' service.

Till now...

He cursed Krobis under his breath, slapped the picture back, face down on the cabinet.

There was another guard at the gate to the Titan ramp. Boone bared his ID plate.

But the man made no move to step aside. "Sorry, Mister

Boone."

"What—?"

"Mister Krobis' orders, sir. You are barred from the ramp till after the ship gravs off."

"Oh." For a long, long moment Boone stood very still. And then: "I see."

"He might still be at his office, sir. Maybe if you was to talk to him…"

"Thanks." Stiffly, Boone turned and walked back the way he'd come, past silent warehouses and noisy shops and rattling, rumbling surface carrier units.

Then he was in front of the blank-faced central administration building.

For the fraction of a second only, he hesitated. Then, turning in, he strode through the deserted passageways.

Krobis' office. Another guard. "Mister Krobis is busy, sir. He left orders that he wasn't to be disturbed till after the Titan ship gravs off."

Again, a long, long moment of decision. Then, very gently, Boone repeated, "I want to see Krobis."

"I'm sorry, sir—"

BOONE brought out the nerve-gun in one swift motion, leveled it at the man's belly. "Maybe you didn't understand."

The guard's eyes flicked from his face to the nerve-gun. "You're making a mistake, sir."

Boone kept the nerve-gun steady, ready. "You're probably right. But anyone who tries to stop me is going to get hurt."

"If that's the way you want it, sir…" The guard shrugged and stepped aside.

"No." Boone shook his head. "You're going in with me, friend. Ahead of me."

Wordless, the guard shrugged again and, turning, walked through the anteroom towards Krobis' door.

Boone spun the nerve-gun's impact dial down to the temporary paralysis level and fired.

The guard crumpled. Stepping across him, Boone tried the door handle.

It was locked.

Sucking in a quick breath, Boone kicked for the bolt with all his might.

The door burst open. He lunged into the office beyond.

It was a big room, with the desk set at the far end so that visitors would have plenty of time to lose self confidence while they walked its length.

Martin Krobis specialized in tricks like that.

He leaped up as Boone came through the door—face stiff, nostrils flaring.

Then: "Boone—!"

"That's right." Boone heeled the door shut behind you. "You're a hard man to see these days, Krobis. This time I couldn't wait."

Krobis straightened slowly, a small, sharp-featured man with too-short legs. Twin spots of color came to mark his cheekbones, and his black eyes grew hard and shiny. "I don't believe I understand you, Boone."

Boone laughed, harsh and bitter. "You understand, all right. He strode forward. "That's why you gave orders to the guards to keep me away from you and off the ramp."

"So—?" This out of a thin-lipped, mask-like face.

"So Eileen Rey doesn't take the Titan run." Boone gestured with the gun. "Let's go, Krobis."

"You realize what you're doing, of course, Boone?" A raw, raging edge crept into Krobis' voice. "You know that this finishes you with IC? That as soon as my report goes in, it's the end of your career?"

Deliberately, Boone spun the nerve-gun's dial to the lethal output point. "Time's too short for talk, Krobis. We're going out to the ramp. You and me, together."

Again, Krobis' nostrils flared. His shoulders drew in. His head thrust a fraction forward.

Boone tightened his finger on the nerve-gun's trigger. "Try

it, Krobis. Just try it."

Silence. Long, aching seconds of silence.

Then, slowly, Krobis' head came up. He made a business of smoothing his sleek black hair and came around the desk, walking with the peculiar, waddling stride that came of trying to stretch his too-short legs farther than they were meant to go.

He hadn't done quite a good enough job on his hairline, either, Boone noted. Tiny beads of sweat still showed at the roots.

"Well, Boone?" Krobis carved the words out of ice.

Stripping a coat from the rack, Boone draped it over his arm to hide the gun, then fell in at Krobis' left, not quite abreast him. In silence, they went through the anteroom where the stunned guard lay and on out of the administration building.

Again, the ramp gate loomed.

Low-voiced, Boone said, "I'm going aboard that Titan ship, Krobis. See that I get there if you want to live."

Krobis didn't answer. But his curt nod took them past the guard.

AHEAD, the great sphere that was the Titan ship glinted under the forspark lights. The cargo hatches were already sealed. The last of the surface carriers shuttled in and out like rumbling beetles through the shadows cast by the stubby tripod legs.

Boone herded Krobis to the loading shaft, into the lift; threw a tight grin at the man on duty. "How long?"

"Seven minutes, sir. We're right on schedule."

"Good enough."

The lift ground upward…halted, finally, deep in the heart of the ship.

Boone prodded Krobis down the narrow, duroid corridor that led to the tech quarters. The card on the last door to the right said, "Miss Rey."

Boone knocked. The tension was almost unbearable now. His palms were slick. His belly quivered.

A latch-click. The door opened part way, framing Eileen's face.

Shoving Krobis ahead of him, Boone crowded her back into the cabin and shouldered shut the door.

She stared. "What——?"

Krobis spoke rapidly, caustically: "Boone's jealous of your new assignment, my dear. He doesn't want to let you go to Titan."

Eileen caught her breath. Her eyes flicked to Boone. "Fred——"

"You can believe that if you want to, Eileen." Boone quit trying to keep the anger, the tension, out of his own voice. "The main thing is, you're not going."

He could see the storm flare in her eyes. "Fred, you can't stop me!"

"Can't I?" Boone tossed the coat from his arm, baring the nerve-gun. "I've watched Krobis run through this big-boss act before, Eileen. He specializes in putting people under obligation. In your case, he knows how much your work means to you, so he'd like to maneuver things around to where you'll feel indebted to him for letting you prove your professional competency at the top level. Only this gun,"——he gestured with it—— "says he's not going to get away with it."

The curves of Eileen's face changed to planes and hollows. A thin white anger-line drew about her mouth. "Fred, this is utterly absurd!"

And from Krobis: "Miss Rey happens to be one of the Cartel's best extraterrestrial biologists——"

Boone slashed in on him: "——And also, at the moment, she's a woman you want." He laughed—savagely, explosively. "A nice coincidence, isn't it? You'd gamble her life on it—send her into a chunk of void where monsters materialize out of nowhere and two ships in three never come back. If she lives and cracks the nut, figures out how those nightmares get aboard our ships and why, mekronal production and your rating—with Eileen and IC both—go sky-high. If she dies, you chalk up another score for yourself as an ironclad Cartel man so set on his job that he doesn't know what sentiment means. Either way, Martin

Krobis wins."

"Then you'd let this ship go out without a biologist?" Eileen's breath came fast and shallow. "You'd let the crew face the monsters with not even a fighting chance to win?"

Boone clipped his words: "Don't worry, there'll be a biologist aboard." And then: "You see—I'm going in your place."

"So—!" Face alight, Krobis turned to Eileen. "I was right, my dear! Boone's jealous, that's all—jealous of you, your ability, the chance I've given you to solve this problem!"

A tremor ran through Eileen. For an instant she swayed, her pale face a mask of mixed emotions.

Then, heedless of the nerve-gun, she clawed at Boone.

He stepped back fast; clubbed his left fist upward.

It caught her squarely on the point of the jaw. Her teeth clicked; her head snapped back. Already sagging, she reeled against the wall, then slid unconscious to the floor.

Krobis started to spin about.

Boone said tightly, "Come ahead, Krobis! Eileen I wouldn't burn. But you—it'd be a pleasure!"

Krobis froze in his tracks.

BOONE shot a quick glance at his chronox. "Less than four minutes till grav-off. We'll have to hurry." He gestured with the nerve-gun barrel. "Get her up!"

"And if I won't?"

"Get her up I said!" Boone's voice rang savage with menace.

Krobis' eyes wavered. Squatting, he dragged Eileen's limp body round till he could slide an arm beneath her and heave her up onto his shoulder.

Boone closed in to help support her. "You know what to tell the man at the lift, Krobis: Miss Rey's suddenly been taken ill, so you're relieving her from duty and assigning me to take her place."

Black eyes asmoulder, Krobis nodded.

"And in case you've got any sharp ideas—just remember no man alive can outrun a nerve charge..." Sliding his hand up under Eileen's service blouse to conceal his weapon, Boone jerked open the cabin door. In seconds, they had Eileen into the lift.

Then they were past the guard...out on the ramp again...into the black shadows on the far side of an emptied cargo carrier.

Boone stepped back while Krobis awkwardly lowered Eileen to the ramp. She moaned a little; that was all.

Barely two minutes till grav-time now, the chronox said.

Krobis straightened. "You'll never get away with this, Boone!" His voice was thick with hate.

"Because you'll stop the grav-off, you mean?" Boone spun the nerve-gun's dial back to the temporary paralysis level. "I've thought of that, too, Krobis."

He squeezed the trigger.

The other's eyes went blank and glassy. He slumped beside Eileen on the ramp.

Pivoting, Boone strode back to the ship.

The hatchmen were already gathering with their sealers. The hum of the converters rose in an all-pervasive drone.

Up in the tech quarters once more, Boone wryly slipped the card bearing Eileen's name from its bracket on the door and substituted his own. Then, going on into the cabin, he threw himself down at full length on the foamex bunk. He was tired, more tired than he could remember ever having been, with the utter weariness that comes of too much strain and tension.

A moment later the signal light above the door flashed red. Then a momentary shifting said that the sphere was off the ground and rising, riding its great beam of anti-gravitational force up from Ganymede's bleak surface.

So it was done. Eileen was safe at last and he, Fred Boone, was on his way to Titan.

Of course, there'd be charges waiting for him when he got back.

If he got back.

Only that could wait. That was still far off in the future.

HE fell asleep that way...a troubled sleep, full of mad, distorted dreams of Eileen and Krobis, and of monsters.

Then, all at once, he was awake again, sitting bolt upright in the bunk—sweat-drenched, fists clenched.

Dimly, confusedly, he sensed that some sound must have roused him.

In the same instant the sound came again—a knock, echoing over-loud in the cabin's stillness.

Stumbling from the bunk, Boone jerked open the door.

Eileen stood in the corridor outside, flanked by two guards with nerve-guns at the ready. A cold-eyed ship's officer waited behind them.

Boone stared—unable to speak, still not quite believing.

"I believe these are my quarters, Mister Boone," Eileen said. She was a picture of chill self-possession. Only a faint trace of color marked the place along her jaw where he had struck her.

"Eileen—!" he choked. "Eileen…"

"You're surprised, you mean?" Her voice stayed icy. "I thought you might be. It's just that you didn't hit me quite as hard as you thought you did. I was conscious again before you ever carried me out of this cabin. But you had a gun, so I let you take me off, then came back on again just behind you."

"I see," Boone nodded slowly. Of a sudden there was a churning weakness in his middle. "Then—Eileen—"

"Miss Rey," she corrected, voice still icy. And then: "You'll understand, of course, that I had no choice but to take this whole thing to the captain."

Again, Boone nodded. "Yes."

"To return to Ganymede once the locks were closed behind us would be an expensive undertaking. So we'll both go on to Titan. I'll serve as biologist for the run, in accordance with my orders. As for you," she said as she shrugged, "your status should be obvious."

"To you, maybe. Not to me."

"Then I'll clarify it." All at once her eyes, her face, mirrored bitter triumph. "You'll make the trip, Mister Boone, but you'll do it as a prisoner—under guard and confined to your quarters!"

CHAPTER TWO

THE captain was a broad-bodied, heavy-shouldered man with the veined red nose and cheeks of a heavy drinker. The cold-eyed way he looked at Boone, low-lidded, told how he felt.

"Don't think I've turned you loose because I like you, Boone," he clipped. "I don't. But we're coming into Saturn's orbit, and that means we need a biologist on duty. Prisoner or not, you qualify, so you're elected."

Boone stared. "Miss Rey—"

"Her temperature hit 104 an hour ago."

A chill ran through Boone. "You mean—"

"That's right. Titan fever."

Boone caught his breath as the door swung open to admit a thin-faced young ensign. "Another down, Captain," the man reported grimly. "Verdov, converter crew."

"That makes four. Thank the good Lord we've got plenty of chandak extract." The captain hunched forward, his thick forearms heavy on the desk. "You see where it puts us, Boone. From here on in it's monster country; we'll pass Japetus any minute. So the quicker you check the ship, the better."

"Right." Dry-lipped, Boone pivoted and strode towards the door, gesturing to the ensign. "Come on."

The other nodded and fell in beside him. "Where do you want to start?"

"Top live cargo section."

Together they rode the lift to the highest level, then walked to the end of the "A" passage.

Boone kicked the hatch of the first bunker. "Open it up."

"Open it—?" The ensign's eyes widened. "You mean you're going to check inside, too?"

Boone nodded curtly. "That's right."

"Well, if you say so…" Frowning, the ensign broke the seal;

swung back the hatch.

Cold air washed over them. Light glinted on the seven-foot synthice slabs stacked floor to ceiling, each casing a contract worker stiff in frozen sleep.

Narrow-eyed, Boone probed each nook and crevice with his light-rod, then stepped back. "All right. Let's have the next one."

The ensign slammed shut the hatch. He studied Boone curiously. "Just what are you looking for?"

Boone shrugged. "Monsters don't come out of nowhere; not really. My bet is that they get aboard our ships at the Titan base—in embryo, maybe, or as a virus. If we can spot one before it's grown to a full-scale nightmare, it may give us a hint as to how to beat them."

"But they say they're human, sometimes—"

"Maybe. But no man I know can appear and disappear at will, and so far we're the only humanoid race we've found anywhere in the system. Till I see more proof, I'll put my money on alien life forms plus optical illusion."

"Oh." The ensign's brows drew together. He opened the next hatch.

Another blank.

It went on like that, section after section. They checked supply storage, power receptors, converters.

Still nothing.

In the control room, when they got there, Japetus was already fading from the visiscreen. Hyperion loomed ahead, a bead-like dot hovering in the shadow of the Rings.

Beyond it, dim and distant, lay Titan.

Titan, greatest satellite of Saturn, nearly half the size of Earth itself. Titan, which had given Man mekronal, the precious, mysterious catalyst that cut loose the human race from the need for the oxygen-nitrogen atmosphere of its homeland.

Titan, world of lost sphere-ships and phantasmic monsters.

Bleakly, Boone wondered if he'd ever reach it.

Or even if he did, would Eileen Rey live to see it with him?

What were the odds against a woman struck down by Titan fever?

Those were questions without answers.

Weary, tight-lipped, he turned from the screen. "Nothing here. Let's try the crew quarters."

"Good enough." Once again, the ensign fell in beside him.

Overhead, the alarm bell clanged.

BOONE went rigid, then spun about as the com-box crackled, raw and ragged: "Top level calling! There's something in "A" passage—something awful! Get the biologist—oh, my God—!"

A scream—the scream of a soul in torment.

The com-box went dead.

The ensign at his heels, Boone raced for the lift-shaft.

The top level, "A" passage. The lights at the far end were out.

Boone snatched the ensign's nerve-gun. Cat-footed, he moved forward.

Ahead, something shifted in the shadows. He became aware of a vague, phosphorescent glow.

A whisper of sound. A floundering wallow of movement.

Raw-nerved, Boone flicked on his light-rod.

Its beam sprayed out across a creature like nothing ever seen before in earth or heaven. A bulbous thing, a nightmare of pseudopodal horror.

But before he could fire, it began to change.

First it drew together, a bubbling mass like green calf-slobber shot with blood. A rank stench of musty death curled to him from it.

Then, while he watched, a shape began to rise out of the slime; a shape—

He caught his breath. His blood froze.

It was a woman!

Now she stood erect and naked, shrouded from the hips down in the slime-mass. Her hands caressed her high, proud breasts. She laughed and stretched her arms out toward Boone.

In spite of himself, he took a dragging step forward. Then another, and another.

As from afar, the ensign's shout dinned in his ears. He half turned.

As one, woman and slime-mass lunged towards him. And now, incredibly, Boone saw that there were fangs beneath the laughing lips; that, like Medusa, the woman was crowned not with rippling hair, but writhing serpents.

He screamed as the voice on the com-box had screamed; blazed point blank at the naked belly with his nerve-gun.

The soft flesh shimmered, darkened. Great scales took form. The smooth body distorted into the plated, cartilaginous torso of a dragon.

Boone hurled himself aside as its great horned head lanced forward. With all his might, he threw the nerve-gun into the yawning mouth.

The mighty jaws damped down. The metal crumpled.

Behind Boone, thunder crashed in the passage. A fire-bolt from a blaster smashed into the monster.

Dragon and slime-mass alike exploded into spattering fragments. Half-stunned, Boone felt the ensign's fingers dig into his shoulders and drag him back towards the lift-shaft.

But he shook them off. "No. I've got to see—" Even as he spoke, he knew that the words were coming out an incoherent mumble.

He staggered back anyhow…clawed amid the smoke and debris. His hands came up green and stinking with viscuous slime.

Numbly, he stared down at them. "Then—it was real—no optical illusion—"

"Real? Of course it was real!" This from the half-hysterical ensign. "I saw it all—the woman, the dragon! If I'd been two seconds later with the blaster, it would have got you!"

Boone slumped against the wall. "That thing—"

A MUFFLED crash of sound from the lift-shaft cut in on him. Red lights flashed on the callboard.

"Third level!" The ensign's voice rang raw with tension.

"Come on!" Boone lunged for the lift.

Together they plummeted downwards...tumbled out into a murky, smoke-eddying third level passage.

More slime, purple this time, and a man with a blaster.

Only he hadn't fired quite quick enough. He sprawled dead on the floor-plates, his chest torn wide open as if by talons.

Red lights were flashing all over the callboard now. Alarm bells jangled wildly.

The captain's voice rasped from the com-box: "All hands! Make for your closest emergency carrier and stand by to abandon ship! Central Control will blow all carriers clear in three minutes! Repeat, Central Control will blow all carriers clear in three minutes, so get aboard fast! All hands..."

Stiff-lipped, Boone stared up at the callboard. "Seven levels signaling! It's an attack in force, then."

The ensign clutched his arm. "Let's go! There's a carrier at the end of the passage!"

Boone started to turn, then stopped short. "Eileen—!"

"What?"

"The other biologist—the girl with Titan fever."

"Let the medmen worry about her! They'll take her off if she's not too sick to move!"

"No!" Spasmodically, Boone jerked free. "We can't leave her!"

"But there's no time!"

"I can't help that." Boone shoved the other away. "You go ahead..."

The ensign threw him one last taut, frustrated glance, then wheeled and ran off down the passage towards the carrier lock. A score of steps he ran...

Only then, out of the murk, a primordial horror rose before him—a thing of tentacles and feelers massed about a hideous white skull-face!

It happened too fast for shouts or screaming. The ensign's head jerked back and sidewise. He tried to veer.

Too late. With a sound that came straight from hell, the skull-thing lurched forward. The tentacles engulfed him.

Convulsively, Boone clawed the blaster from the dead hands of the man beside the lift-shaft...lanced a fire-bolt into the monster's leering face.

Face and monster vanished in a blaze of ear-shattering sound and blue-white flame.

Then the echoes died and Boone was alone again—shaking, retching. Of the ensign, no trace remained.

NUMBLY, Boone stumbled back into the lift and dropped it full speed down the shaft to the tenth level, the very heart of the great sphere-ship.

There was another monster waiting for him when he came out—a creature that looked for all the world like a huge, iridescent coffin whose lid came up to bare rows of razor-edged shark-teeth.

Raw-nerved, he blasted it to atoms; then, belly churning, waded through stench and putrescent fragments towards the tech quarters where Eileen lay.

As he did so, the ship rocked sharply.

For an instant Boone went rigid, then cursed aloud. That jolt—it could have been only the impact of the carriers' departure.

Now, truly, he was alone—alone in the void on a sphere of death, where nightmare monsters roamed lusting for his blood.

Alone with Eileen, perhaps. If she were still alive.

If...

He quickened his pace, moving along the corridor cold-eyed and wary, his finger taut on the blaster's trigger.

The last door to the right. A card that said, "Miss Rey."

Palm slick with sweat, Boone tried the handle.

The door was unlocked. He opened it a fraction.

A voice rose high and incoherent, ranting. The voice of delirium.

Boone stepped inside; flicked on the light.

Eileen lay in the bunk, held there by the broad straps of a safety pack. A flush-faced Eileen with wild, fever-blinded eyes. Her lips moved in ceaseless, garbled speech. Thin fingers tugged and twisted at the sheets as if it were not in them to be still.

A knot drew tight in Boone's midriff. Grimly, he studied the chart on the stand, then glanced at his chronox.

Time for more chandak extract. Stiff-fingered, he prepared the aerojet; sprayed the precious drops into Eileen's jugular vein. Then, barring the door against invading monsters, he settled down to wait and hope.

The hours dragged by till he lost track, a blur of time broken only by the routine with the aerojet. Once he thought Eileen recognized him. Twice he fell asleep. A dozen times, in his mind's eye, the monsters came, only to fade away again as he fought his way up from the depths of his fatigue. Hunger, thirst—they were words only...

Then, the crash.

It threw him clear across the cabin, to land with stunning force against the farthest wall. The whole room hung tilted at a thirty-degree angle.

Dragging himself up, he clambered to the bunk.

Eileen's eyes were closed, her tongue and fingers still at last. To Boone it seemed as if her forehead were less feverish—as if she might even be asleep.

But again, she might have slipped into a coma. In his own state, he couldn't be sure.

As for the crash, the room... Blinking, he looked around.

The cabin's angle was still the same. Thirty degrees, at least.

Only the room couldn't stay this way, tilted. Not with the sphere floating free in space. That was what the orientational gyroscopes were designed to prevent.

In the same instant, he caught the first faint whiff of ammonia.

A chill ran through him. Scrambling erect, he snatched up the blaster, fumbled open the door, and peered out into the corridor.

No monsters—but something worse. For here the ammonia smell hung even stronger.

DRAGGING the door shut behind him. Boone half-ran half-fell along the crazily tilted passage to the administrative center at the ship's core.

The door to the medical office was locked. Cursing savagely, Boone drew back and to one side and fired a glancing bolt.

The door swung wide, the lock and half the panel shattered.

Inside, Boone pawed the supply chest into chaos, then turned to the wall cabinets.

A case of mekronal ampules stood on the first shelf.

Coughing as a new eddy of ammonia fumes curled round him, Boone snatched down the carton and an extra aerojet injector, then ran from the room and back along the passage to Eileen's cabin.

The air inside was a little better. Slamming shut the door, he tossed down the ampules and began wadding the first of Eileen's garments to come to hand into the wall vent.

A faint voice whispered, "Fred..."

Boone spun around. "Eileen—!"

She smiled, the pale wraith of a smile. But her eyes had lost their fever-wildness. Her cheeks were no longer quite so flushed.

"What's...the matter, Fred?"

"Nothing. Nothing." Futilely, Boone groped for some assuring fable. "It's just—you've been down with Titan fever—"

"Don't...lie to me, Fred. Please tell me." And then, "Were there...monsters—?"

All of a sudden Boone could no longer face her. "Yes, there were monsters." He pivoted; stuffed more clothing into the air vent. "All hands took off in carriers. Now the ship's crashed—

on Hyperion, maybe; someplace with an ammonia—and—methane atmosphere, anyhow. The plates must have sprung when we hit. The smudge outside is leaking in."

"Then—what—?"

Boone finished with the vent. Sliding down to the bunk, he tore open the mekronal case with unsteady fingers; drew out an ampule.

"We'll try it on mekronal," he answered in a voice gone flat in spite of him. "If we can last three hours till it takes effect, we still may make it."

He readied the injector and sprayed the ampule's contents into Eileen's bloodstream, then shot a second into his own.

The girl's hand touched his; held it. "I'm...so tired..." Her eyes closed

She slept.

Seconds dragging by, melding into minutes. The cabin growing uncomfortably warm, the air stale and stuffy.

A half-hour gone. Time for another ampule.

Again and again, Boone read the legend on the carton: *Mekronal is an unanalyzed catalyst derived from the skeletal structure of the non-carbon chemistry life form* Helgae *found on Titan. When injected into the human bloodstream, it enables man to breathe all known atmospheres, regardless of content, without toxic effect. Dosage: One ampule every thirty minutes till three ampules have been injected. Repeat weekly until return to normal oxygen-nitrogen atmosphere. Takes effect within approximately three hours after first injection though an additional one-hour safety factor is recommended.*

"Takes effect within approximately three hours after first injection..."

Three endless hours.

Or the other line—"Enables man to breathe all known atmospheres, regardless of content, without toxic effect."

Did that include carbon dioxide atmospheres like the one now forming in this cabin?

Bleakly, Boone wondered. He checked his chronox.

Time for the third injection.

Maybe it would be better to take no chances—move Eileen to a lower point, where the air was clearer.

Besides, the heat here by the bunk was becoming almost unbearable. Already, both of them were drenched with sweat.

Sweat! Heat—! Boone went rigid.

There shouldn't be any heat to speak of—not if they lay in a plate-sprung ship on Hyperion's frigid surface!

Then what—?

Boone could find no ready answer.

The air grew thicker, thicker. Eileen's breathing steadily became more labored.

FREEING her from the safety pack, Boone carried her to the room's lowest corner. She roused a little, then sank back once more, as if even consciousness had become an effort.

More seconds. More minutes.

Then, slowly, the pressure on Boone's lungs seemed to lift. Depression and weariness fell away. New energy flowed through him.

He dared a look at his chronox, three hours and seventeen minutes!

Suddenly he was giddy with exaltation. He wanted to shout, to laugh and leap.

From the corner, Eileen whispered, "Fred, have we made it?"

Wordless, he stumbled to her.

Her eyes were open, cool and steady. The last flushed traces of fever had vanished.

"Eileen—!" he choked, "Eileen…" and strained her to him.

Then, because he could not trust his own emotions further, he rose and took up the blaster. "I'll go take a look around, get you something to eat."

The corridor outside was thick with the alien atmosphere. But though it stung his eyes a little, his lungs now accepted it without protest.

Watchful, wary of monsters, he made his way to the galleys

and gathered up a sack of food, wolfing down a whole can of meat synthetic in the process.

Eileen was up and dressed when he returned. Grinning, he watched her eat with the eager hunger of the fever-famished.

When she had finished and he got up to leave again, she rose also. "Fred, I'm going with you."

He shook his head. "You're too weak. You need to take it easy."

"Please, Fred."

For an instant his eyes met hers and he knew again that now, as always, he never could deny her. "All right. Just for a little way."

Together, his arm about her, they left the cabin…turned down the corridor that led to the nearest carrier lock.

The hatch hung free, sprung from its hinges. Bracing himself, Boone levered it open.

Eileen caught her breath. "Fred—!"

He twisted; stared out past her.

The sight that met his eyes set his senses reeling.

For here lay no frozen wastes, no icy crags and barrens.

Instead, a blaze of living color spread before him, kaleidoscopic in its brilliance. Huge flowers—like none that he had ever seen—carpeted the foreground in clumps of yellow, red, green, purple—every color of the rainbow. Strange trees stretched upward towards the shining blue vault of the sky, rustling and swaying in the gentle breeze.

"Fred—!" Eileen's hand rested on his shoulder. "Fred, it's beautiful!"

Her words broke the spell. "Beautiful? Yes, of course it is," Boone nodded, frowning. "But the question is, where are we? There's no planet like this anywhere in our whole solar system, so far as I know—"

He broke off; moved out into the carrier cradle proper, where he could get a broader field of vision.

To the right, the flowerland stretched away to rolling hills that spread as far as he could see.

To the left.—

He went rigid.

Beyond the flower-fields, strange, low domes rose—gray-silver domes whose very lines and curves bespoke an alien pattern. One atop the other they piled in a jumbled, sprawling mass like bubbles trapped in cooling lava. Boone could only guess how many miles of ground they covered.

Yet it was a scene of a kind he'd seen before, once, on microreels in IC's confidential archives.

Behind him, Eileen caught her breath. "Those things—Fred, are they buildings?"

"Buildings?" Boone hesitated; fumbled. "I don't know. I guess that you might call them that."

"You guess—? Then you recognize them!" Eileen's blue eyes were suddenly worry-shadowed. "Tell me, Fred. Don't hold back. Is something wrong? Where are we?"

For a long, long moment Boone stared away at the distant dome-pile. "No, nothing's wrong," he said at last. "Maybe it's even better luck than we could hope for…but wherever we are, Eileen, one thing's for certain…that place is a Helgae city!"

CHAPTER THREE

IT was a situation that held Boone tense, uneasy.

On the one hand, the Helgae domes loomed over the paradisiacal flower-land where the sphere-ship lay in strange, silent menace.

On the other, aboard the globe, he could not but chill to the recollection of the monsters.

As for Eileen...Boone wondered. She had said not a word about their earlier trouble—his desperation-born effort to keep her from making the Titan run; its sudden reversal and her triumph. Yet after the first moments of tenderness and relief at their own survival, the clash hung like an invisible wall between them. Out of it, a reserve had come into being—a weighing of words, a wary watching.

Or was that only his imagination?

Regardless, they had to adjust to each other's presence, to work out some solution to their mutual problem.

Cautious exploration finally convinced him that the monsters had vanished from the ship as mysteriously as they'd come. It didn't surprise him; it had been the pattern in every such invasion—nightmare figures materializing out of the void to wreak chaos aboard the IC's Titan-bound craft, then disappearing again; back into whatever dark limbo they called home.

Too, the carrier towards which the dead ensign had been running when the monster seized him was still aboard; apparently the blast-charge had jammed its locks. So there was at least a slim chance for escape.

It was enough for Boone. He persuaded Eileen that, weak as she was, it would be best to stay in her cabin and eat and sleep and rest while they waited for night and stars that might give them some clue as to where they were.

For his own part, he moved from one empty carrier cradle to another, studying the landscape and the sky.

The effort brought only bafflement. Here and there in the distance, great mountains towered. But always, the blue of the heavens seemed to chop off their highest peaks, as if the sky were a translucent ceiling that they pierced.

Nor could he find the sun, save as a vague, luminous glow that shifted slowly towards the far horizon.

Yet the astrogation micro reels showed no satellite or planet short of Venus with an atmosphere thick enough to give such an effect.

Then, at last, the light began to fade. Eagerly, Boone waited for the stars.

Instead, a pitch-black night came down. Only in one tiny spot, almost directly over the fallen globe-ship, could he detect a spark of light.

Then it, too, vanished.

Boone cursed aloud.

But when, once again, he scanned the sky, the spark was back where it had been.

Or was it? Before, the glint had shone cold and blue. Now, it seemed to have a faint orange cast.

He settled down to watching it, as nearly without blinking as he could.

For a few minutes it grew brighter, then faded again till only ebony black remained.

Still Boone held his eyes on the place where it had been.

A dim, greenish glow, so pale he could not be sure that it was really there. Then a pinprick of undeniable light.

Minutes, ticking by.

A rustle of movement. At his elbow, Eileen said, "Fred, that light—this black—I don't understand."

"I'm afraid I do." Boone rubbed the stiffness from his neck and quit trying to watch the spark above. "We've always thought of the outer worlds as rock and ice. Where this one's concerned, we were wrong. There's ice, all right, but at least in places it's just a shell, with a warm pocket underneath."

He could hear Eileen's breath hiss in the darkness. "Then you mean—"

"Yes. We must have been crossing this planetoid's orbit when the crew abandoned ship. It's too small to have much gravity, but there was enough to pull us in. So we crashed through the ice-shell and landed here."

THE girl's body touched his. He could feel her shiver. "Then those lights we see are the stars as they pass above the hole we made? We'll have to go through it again to get back into space?"

"That's right." Boone put his arm about her shoulders. "It shouldn't be too hard. I'm betting this is Hyperion—and that means we are close enough to jump to Titan, even in a carrier. We'll know for sure when it gets light again. I can check the time from sunset to sunrise against the tables that show how long it takes Hyperion to revolve on its axis."

"You make it seem so easy." Eileen sighed. "In a way, I'm not even sure I want to go."

"That has a nice sound." Boone held her closer.

But she twisted. "No. It—it isn't what you think, Fred."

Boone let his arm fall. He frowned into the darkness. "Then why—?"

"Can't you guess?" All at once the girl sounded weary, almost bitter. "There's going to be trouble, Fred. Trouble with Krobis. You know that."

"Oh."

"He won't forget what you did. He'll break you for it. And—and I won't like that."

"You...won't like it?"

"You know I won't. You—you saved my life."

Boone could feel his muscles tensing. In spite of him, his voice came edged: "Then that's all that's bothering you? You just don't want to see me get in trouble?"

"No, no! —Oh, I don't know!" Eileen's words were

suddenly stumbling and uneven. "It's just that—well, you showed me something, Fred, when you tried to stop me. How you feel about me. How my work doesn't really matter to you."

"I see." Boone's mood turned raw and savage. "Maybe you even figure like Krobis pretended he did—that I was just jealous of your assignment when I barged into this business."

"Fred!" she exclaimed. "You're trying to hurt me. I know I hurt you…I know…so now you want to pay me back."

He didn't answer.

A moment of silence. At last Eileen said, "I—I think I'll go to bed. I'm still awfully tired. That fever…"

Her voice trailed away. Then, after another moment, her shoes whispered on the cradle-plates.

Still Boone stared bleakly out into the darkness.

The whispering footsteps faded, then died. He stood alone, in utter silence. Even the murmur of the breeze in the trees about the ship was stilled.

That stillness—it made him frown a little—wasn't natural, somehow.

As a matter of fact, was anything natural in this weird, ice-shelled wonderland? Even the flowers lacked kinship with those he'd known on Earth.

Or did they?

It came to him in a flash that what he needed now was action. The night, the silence, the bitter disillusion—they'd rasped his nerves in a raw tension. Unless he cut it loose, something would snap. The flowers, then, could serve as an outlet.

First, he'd get a light-rod…

Pivoting, he strode back along the carrier guides to the hatch…started to step through.

From the other side came the hiss of a quick-drawn breath.

Boone froze. "Eileen…"

A tremulous laugh. "Fred, I came back. I—I was afraid."

"Oh." He made it curt. "I'm going out as soon as I can find a light."

"I've got one." A beam blazed in the black, half-blinding him. She looked at him, puzzled. "You're going—out—?"

"Yes. Down to the ground. I want a closer look at some of those flowers."

It was a belligerent statement, geared for more trouble. But Eileen's tone stayed almost humble:

"Can I come with you?"

"If you want to." Boone took the light-rod and, with no further words, led the way down to the sphere-ship's lowest level and out through another carrier-cradle.

JUST short of the mouth, he paused. Lowering himself carefully from the cradle-lip, he tested the ground.

It had the slightly spongy feel of thick carpeting, but there was no question but that it would hold his weight. Spraying the light out in a quick arc, he checked for other dangers—of just what sort he wasn't sure—and then helped Eileen down.

Already he felt better, perhaps even a trifle chagrined at the emotions that had brought him here.

But it wasn't in him to show that now. Crossing to the nearest flower-clump, he spread the petals of a half-opened bud.

They were gigantic—three times the size of any he'd ever seen before. Within the corolla lay half-a-dozen concentric rings of threadlike, sharply differentiated tendrils.

He frowned; spoke half to himself: "Which are the stamens?"

"Or are there any?" Eileen slid a fingernail across the rippling tendrils. "Maybe this is a different kind of plant than we know—one based on six sexes instead of two."

"Maybe." Still frowning, Boone picked another flower to study. Again, as earlier up in the carrier-cradle, he was acutely conscious of the blackness pressing in about them, the utter silence. It brought a queer prickling along his spine.

Eileen brushed against him. "Fred, why can't we let this wait till morning? After all, what do we know about this place, or the Helgae?" There was a tremor in her voice.

"The Helgae?" Stubbornly, Boone shrugged off his own mood. "If they could do anything to humans, they'd have done it when IC started operations out on Titan. As for this place—" He tilted the light-rod up to illuminate the ground ahead.

Its beam stopped short a bare six feet before them, cut off as completely as by a wall.

Eileen clutched his arm. "Fred—!"

Boone whipped the beam left.

Six feet it carried, no more. Whirling, he pointed it back in the direction from which they had come, squarely at the sphere-ship.

But there was no ship; or if there was, the light-beam could not reach it.

Panic gripped Boone—the black, surging panic that roars up in a tidal wave when Man stands face to face with the unknown. Dimly, he knew that Eileen had swayed against him, that instinctively he'd thrown his arm about her. That was all.

Yet in spite of it, now he forced himself into striding forward—one creaking step…two…three…

The light-beam shortened with each step.

The truth dawned on him, then: The beam stopped short as if cut off by a wall…because, indeed, a wall had risen up before it!

A dull, translucent wall of silvery gray.

Numbly, he lanced the beam skyward.

There, too, it broke on the Grey shell.

Boone's panic channeled into fury. He spun about; struck savagely at the barrier.

Blood spurted from split knuckles. The wall remained.

Twisting, he hurled his full weight against the barrier.

Again, it threw him back.

He straightened, then; swung round the light-rod, searching the shell for some flaw, some weakness.

He found none.

Beside him, Eileen was sobbing, "Fred, what's happened?"

"What's happened—?" Boone laughed, a harsh and bitter

laugh. "We're trapped, Eileen…that's what. Trapped in a Helgae bubble like those domes we saw!"

Her tears died. She stared at him. "But the Helgae can't hurt humans—"

"They can't?" He threw out the query like a challenge. "What do we really know about it?"

"But—on Titan—"

"On Titan, we found what we thought was a dead or dying culture. No one's ever seen Helgae alive. Or maybe we have. They're a non-carbon chemistry life form. The elemental blobs we figured for skeletal structure may actually be their version of organic matter. Our mekronal units could have been smashing the golden age of their civilization, for all we really know."

The girl's face blanched. "No! It can't be!"

"Why can't it?" Her opposition lashed Boone to new fierceness. "Man's never found a way to communicate with any other life form—not even on our own home planet! We can't talk to ants or paramecium, let alone Martian torglors or Callistan crustachs. But we're egoists, so we've taken it for granted we're the only truly intelligent creatures. All over the system, we've moved in at will, taken what we wanted, because we had the power to do it. But maybe the Helgae are different. Maybe, on their plane, they can think as well as we do, or better. Do you think they won't react when the Cartel rips apart their cities and hauls them off by millions for the sake of the mekronal that can be extracted from their bodies?"

EILEEN drew back. Her eyes distended. "You're mad, Fred! The Helgae—they'd strike back if they were alive or had the power to think!"

"Maybe they have. Maybe that's the origin of Titan fever, and the monsters that appear aboard our sphere-ships." Boone hammered on the shell that caged them. "Or would you like to deny this bubble, too? Whether it came down from above or grew up from below, it's here—and I, for one, can't break it!"

Eileen's lips were quivering. Her face averted. Her

shoulders shook. "Fred—oh, Fred…"

Then she was crumpling. Barely in time, Boone caught her; held her.

What was there in him that made him strike out so at her? Jealously, as Krobis said? Frustration at their plight here? A projection of the rage he felt towards himself for having been fool enough to leave the security of the sphere-ship to come out here in the black night without decent reason?

Or was it as some forgotten poet had said in a line of verse that he remembered— "For each man kills the thing he loves…"

He cursed aloud.

The night dragged on, with Boone cradling the girl in his arms. There were no more words between them.

Then pale light came, filtered and dim within the Gray translucence of the bubble. Eileen roused, suddenly wild-eyed and rigid. "Fred—"

"Easy, girl. We're still inside the bubble." And then, to soothe her: "Don't worry. They wouldn't have taken the trouble to make us prisoners if they'd planned to kill us right away."

She didn't answer.

Wearily, Boone got up and started towards the shell's closest wall.

But as he did so, the ground seemed to come alive beneath his feet. Crackling and crumbling it tilted so sharply that he was pitched from his feet.

Then earth and flower-sod alike were sliding. Loose loam cascaded over Boone. Desperately, he tried to find Eileen amid the welter.

"Here, Fred! Behind you!"

Floundering, Boone craned to see her.

She stood close to the shell's wall, braced against it.

Then another trembler threw him flat; half-buried him.

Clawing, cursing, he wallowed towards the girl.

She darted forward in the same instant. Her hand locked on

his. With a final effort he shook free of the clods and lurched panting to a place at the wall beside her.

Another jolt. Again the earth slipped from beneath his feet. Yet now, since he had the wall to brace him, the surge of movement did not fell him.

Then it dawned on him that the shell itself was sliding, sliding upwards!

It was Eileen who gave the answer: "Lean back, Fred! The bubble's rolling, that's all. The dirt keeps sliding forward." Strangely, her voice was steady now…calm, almost.

After that, there was no more time for talking. Faster and faster, the Gray sphere careened onward, bumping and bouncing. A dozen times, one or the other of them fell. But as long as they held their places against the rear wall, the earth and clods spilled away from them, so that with sweat and scrambling they managed each time to regain their footing.

Then, at long last, the strange globe slowed and changed direction. The surface beneath it seemed smoother now, and the bubble moved in arcs and curves. Shadows fell across it. The light grew dim, then faded altogether.

More movement, through long lanes of utter darkness. Strange sounds, faint whispers in the stillness.

Then, abruptly, light again—a blaze of it, dazzling and incandescent.

The bubble halted.

A crash of silent thunder, more felt than heard.

Its impact pitched Boone and Eileen forward into the dirt. The globe split into segments like a quartered orange.

Half-stunned, they stared about.

IT was a chamber such as Boone had never seen before—a great, bare bubble-room whose very walls radiated chill white light.

Lurching to his feet, he stumbled down from the tumbled earth.

Two steps he took. And then, incredibly, he could go no

further, for out of nowhere, a new bubble, crystal clear and barely large enough for him to stand erect, had formed around him.

He spun about.

Like him, Eileen stood in a solitary global prison. Stiff-faced with fear, she gestured to him—helpless, hopeless.

He hammered at the shimmering wall in furious frenzy. But to no avail. The casing gave no more than had that of the cell in which he and Eileen had come.

His sphere began to move away from Eileen's, then. Like a huge ball it rolled, spinning out in an arc that carried it through some unseen exit that led from the chamber of chill white light.

Then...darkness again.

But only briefly, this time. Then, once more, the globe halted. New light came, a warm and golden glow.

Again, Boone peered forth.

Now he lay in a sort of amphitheater, it seemed—a bubble joined on all sides by a thousand other, smaller bubbles.

Each lesser sphere held one of the Helgae.

Fascinated, Boone studied them through the clear walls of his cage; and never did man look on stranger creatures.

For their bodies were mottled, shapeless blobs—limbless, with no visible trace of sensory organs. They could as well have been lumps of mud or metal, for all that Boone could see.

Perhaps the men at the Titan base had been right. It outraged human reason even to dream that such things could have intelligent, independent life.

Only then an alien thought flashed through Boone's mind—a thought without meaning, couched in terms no mammalian brain could ever have defined.

Boone groped; floundered. Another thought-tendril reached him, even less translatable than the first. He felt an uneasiness, a twinge almost of conscience, as if this were a thing that duty demanded he should grasp.

But effort made no slightest difference. Though he strained till his temples throbbed, the concept remained beyond his powers to understand.

Shaking, he gripped his head between his hands.

Now the patterns came in dozens, hundreds. Boone's brain reeled under their impact. He staggered, then cried out in helpless fury.

As swiftly as they had come, the alien intellects withdrew.

Weak, drenched with sweat, Boone slumped to the bottom of his sphere.

As he did so, the golden glow that bathed him changed to deepest purple.

Taut, eyes flickering, Boone watched and waited.

Slowly, a new sensation came.

This time, there was no alien thought-projection—if, indeed, it had been that which he had felt before.

Rather, now, the other minds were probing his own brain-cells—searching his cortex with tendrils a thousand times more delicate than Man's finest nerve-ends; wringing out his thoughts as one might squeeze water from a sponge. There was a laying-bare of dreams dredged from the deep subconscious, a draining off of skills and knowledge.

And agony came with it—an agony that rose from soul, not body; a pain that seared beyond all human ken. Through a thousand years it stretched, that pain—a thousand years when seconds lasted eons.

Boone writhed and screamed. At least, he thought he did. For never, never, so long as he should live, could he be quite sure.

Yet he knew, somehow, that, lacking a universe of discourse, the things the Helgae sought most were still locked in his brain. Like him, they could not bridge the chasm that yawned between such different minds.

Then it was over and the glow of purple, too, was fading. The probing minds drew back their tendrils. Boone's sphere dissolved into a place of glorious, delirium-born darkness and he was falling…falling…

CHAPTER FOUR

IT was a wondrous world. He walked in halls of polished marble and looked out through colonnades across a bright blue sea. Gentle breezes carried flowers' perfumes to him. Wine warmed his throat. Music rippled in faint, nostalgic waves.

Yet he knew no joy, for loneliness ached dull underneath his breastbone. First listless, then feverish, he wandered in and out among the columns, ever seeking. Servitors brought rare foods, sun-blushing fruits, to tempt his palate; and there were women who pressed themselves upon him, seducing him with eye and voice and touch.

But he brushed by; he would have none of them. He saw the blue sea as a wasteland. The wine turned bitter in his mouth.

Then, suddenly, *she* was there, a fairy figure far off amid the towering pillars. With a glad cry, he ran towards her.

But she laughed and flitted away before him. And when he tried to follow, dusk came, casting ebon shadows, and he could not find her, and he threw himself down on the hard bed of the marble, bruised and broken.

"Eileen—!" he moaned. "Eileen…"

As from afar, a voice said, "That's right. Another shot of vorghon."

He turned his head, ever so slowly. He forced his burning, heavy-lidded eyes to open.

A man in the white jacket of the medcorps stood beside him, smiling. "Good," the man said. "I knew we'd do it. Vorghon always brings them around."

"You hit it, all right." It was another medman speaking. "For awhile there, I'd begun to wonder. But that last shot turned the trick."

Again Boone whispered: "Eileen—where is she?"

"Eileen, did you say? The first of the medmen came down

closer. "Some girl? You were alone, you know, aboard the carrier."

"The...carrier—?"

"You don't remember that part, even?" The medman's brow furrowed deeper. His eyes flicked to his fellow for the fraction of a second as if in wordless exclamation, then came back to Boone again. "You were aboard a sphere-ship bound for Titan. Then the monsters hit it and all hands took off. When we picked you up, you were in an EC carrier, drifting just out of Hyperion's orbit." He chuckled. "You were out of your head at the time. Someplace along the line you'd gotten pretty sick."

Boone tried to drag himself up but found his arms were pinioned. "I was on Hyperion," he mumbled. "I didn't leave the ship; it crashed down through the ice-shell. Eileen was with me—"

But the medman had straightened. He was not listening. "Another shot for this lad," he clipped briskly. "Make it equal parts of vorghon and anhalsax."

"Right, sir," the second medman nodded. Boone glimpsed an aerojet descending.

Then he was off again—off on another nightmare chase, following Eileen through sifting spheres of light and darkness.

This time, at last, he caught her. Only when he would have put his arms about her, she suddenly changed into a faceless, somehow leering Helgae.

But the haze was gone when he roused again, and he felt better.

Then the medmen came in, looking not quite so jovial as before. A frozen-faced ship's officer entered with them.

There was the usual routine check. At its conclusion, the medman in charge turned to the officer. "All right. You can talk to him now." He stepped back.

THE officer moved in closer.

"Your name's Fred Boone, EB rating, attached to the Ganymedan base." He said it as if it were an accusation.

"That's right."

"On September 3, 2156, adjusted Earth dating system, you forced the base director, Martin Krobis, to pass you onto the base grav-ramp, then paralyzed him with a nerve-shock and stowed away aboard sphere-ship XL-23°, bound for Titan, in direct violation of his specific orders."

Boone studied the officer thoughtfully, but said nothing.

"Well?"

"Well what?"

The officer's ears grew pink. "Affirm or deny."

"I'd rather not do either 'til I have advice of counsel."

"Oh, one of those." The officer's lips drew tight. "All right, then, if that's the way you want it. But I warn you, it won't help you."

Turning on his heel, he stalked out the door. The medmen followed.

Still Boone lay unmoving. There was a tension in him now, and of a sudden he felt old and weary.

So even here, even now, after all that had happened, Krobis was bound to get his pound of flesh.

Almost idly, he wondered how it would end.

Not that it mattered. Not now, with Eileen still back on Hyperion, a captive of the Helgae.

If she'd lived this long.

Bleakly, he wondered what had happened that day—or was it night?—in the weird domed city. Were the Helgae living entities, as it had seemed? Had they really tried to probe his brain by some strange thought-wave system? Or was that all imagination?

For that matter, had he ever actually been beneath the ice-shell? Did it even exist? And was there a warm, lush world inside it—a world where huge, six-sexed flowers bloomed and held their colors in spite of ammonia and methane; where Helgae bubbles formed in a flash to trap invaders?

Above all, how had he come to be aboard a carrier, drifting be yond Hyperion's orbit?

Those were questions to which, some day, he'd have to find the answers.

Such questions—and so many of them.

Yet in his heart he knew that they were academic, almost. For they only concealed the true core of his tension.

Eileen.

Again he saw her as in those last long moments—sealed in her separate sphere, her pale face fear-straught.

The memory woke new fever in him. Why was he lying here, with her in danger? Now, above all, seconds were precious.

And there was only one road for him to take to help her.

A bitter road. Yet he had no choice.

He shifted; twisted; fumbled for the buzzer button.

A medman came. Boone said, "I want a space-phone."

"Who are you calling?"

"The Ganymedan base director. His name is Martin Krobis."

"I'll see." The man went out again.

When he came back, he brought an audio-visual com-box with him. "The call's allowed. I've placed it for you." Setting down the unit on the stand beside Boone's bed, he left the room.

Taut-nerved, Boone waited.

Then the signal blinked. Krobis' face flashed on the receptor screen sharp features set in an expression that was half gloating smirk, half chill, bleak menace. "Well, Boone?" His voice came brittle.

Boone hunched forward. "Let's, not waste time on things past Krobis. We know how we feel about each other. What counts now is that Eileen's in trouble."

Tersely, he told his story.

But Krobis' expression stayed the same. The black eyes showed no slightest flicker of emotion.

"That's all, Boone?"

Boone's palms were sweating, "That's all—?" he echoed. "Isn't that enough? What more do you want."

FOR the first time, Krobis' facial muscles shifted. Hate boiled in his eyes. His lips peeled back in a raging grimace. "I want you, Boone!" he slashed out fiercely. "I want you, and I'm going to get you! Before I'm through, you'll be booted out of Cartel service and rubbing *djec* in Venus barracks. This nonsense you've told me," he laughed—a harsh, contemptuous laugh, "do you think I don't see through it? Not even a cadet on his first trip would swallow it! You're trying to save your own neck, that's all. But it won't work, not for a minute—"

"But Eileen—"

"To hell with her, too! Even if I believed you, my job's in Mekronal, not Rescue Service."

He broke off sharply, as if unable to find words harsh enough to vent his fury. His hand blurred as he flicked the switch.

The screen went dead.

Belly quivering, Boone turned off his own unit and slumped back on the bed.

But before he could even sort out his own feelings, the combox signal blinked again.

For the fraction of a second Boone hesitated, nonplussed and frowning, then threw the switch.

This time the face on the screen was one he hadn't seen before: a stern-faced man with graying hair, all dignity.

The other said, "I'm Douglas Schilling, specialist in space law at Thelema. A mutual friend heard about your current difficulties. He suggested that you might like to have me serve as counsel."

Boone stared. "A mutual friend—"

"Yes," Schilling nodded. "He prefers that I not use his name over the space-phone, but he said you'd remember him as the man to whom you were talking in Gandor City just before you left for Titan."

Gandor City—! Boone rocked. That could only be Terral, the representative of Associated Independents!

"Do you remember?" Schilling prodded.

Boone made his face a mask. "Yes. I remember."

"Then if you'd care to have me represent you—"

"I would." Boone leaned back and smiled thinly. "That is, if you're still willing after you've heard my story. Krobis has already turned it down."

"Krobis—" The other's keen eyes flickered. "You mean you've talked to him, given him the details as to what happened?"

"Yes."

"I can't say that I'm glad to hear it. However..." The lawyer shrugged. "Let's make it that I'll see you when your ship gravs down at the Cartel's Thelema headquarters base on Mars tomorrow."

"Good enough."

"Till tomorrow, then..." Already, the lawyer's face was fading.

TOMORROW. To Boone, it seemed that the hours dragged on beyond measure. Yet then, when at last the new day had come, he found himself almost regretful—dreading the things he knew that it must bring; fighting down an ever-growing tension.

Because he knew in his heart that he wasn't going to take it. Not with Eileen's life perhaps at stake; not with Hyperion's ice-shell beckoning.

Somewhere, somehow, he'd find a way...

There was a final routine with the medmen. They pronounced him sound, turned him over to the guards.

Then the ship slowed, hovered. Gravving down through the great Thelema airlocks, it settled to the ramp.

Flanked by two guards, Boone strode from the lift-shaft.

Schilling stood outside. Coolly, he extended documents to Boone's captors. "A temporary order for release of your prisoner to my custody for pre-hearing consultation, gentlemen."

The guard in charge checked through the papers, then stepped back. "He's all yours, Mister."

Schilling led the way to a surface carrier without speaking.

Boone eyed him curiously. "How does it look?"

The lawyer leaned back, and the carrier slid smoothly into motion. "Frankly, I don't like it. Krobis wants blood. He's come in all the way from Ganymede himself, instead of sending a deposition or testifying on the com-box; and he's persuaded the Cartel to try you before a general board so that you can be discharged from the service, with release to the Federation for criminal action if you're convicted."

"So it's double trouble." Boone smiled wryly. "I might have expected that from Krobis."

"You're not convicted yet," retorted Schilling. "Besides, I got that release order so you'd have a chance to talk with someone who's in a spot to help you."

"Terral?"

The lawyer nodded and brought the carrier to a halt beside a building. "You'll find him in my office, there. I'll drop back later."

It was Boone's turn to nod. He got out and went into the building.

And there was Terral—lean, gray, shrewd-eyed Terral, the man empowered to speak for Associated Independents.

He gripped Boone's hand. "Glad to see you, man—even though the circumstances could be better."

"Oh, I don't know." Boone held face and voice alike noncommittal. "Anyhow, thanks for getting Schilling."

"You're wondering why, of course." Terral's lips drew thin. "Believe me, it wasn't altruism, Boone; not one bit of it."

Boone frowned. "Maybe I just don't understand."

"You will," the other clipped. And then: "Boone, how much do you know about Titan fever?"

"Titan fever—?" Boone shook his head. "Not too much."

"Are you aware that it's reached the epidemic stage on half-a-dozen satellites and planets?"

"What—!"

"The Federation's keeping the statistics under cover; otherwise there'd be a panic." Terral paced the floor like a caged lion. "The catch is, Boone, we're all like you: No one knows too much about the whys and wherefores of it, except that the original cases came among IC men who worked in the Helgae cities on Titan back when mekronal was first developed."

BOONE ran his thumb along his chin. "I'd heard that part. But I thought we had it licked with chandak extract."

"Chandak extract!" The Independents' agent spun around, gray eyes blazing. "That's just the trouble! Chandak's a byproduct of mekronal—and all mekronal comes from Titan. So with IC assigned monopoly rights there, the rest of us are stuck."

"But the Federation—"

"The Federation's run by blithering idiots and IC stooges. Sure, with this epidemic they've set up a quota system. But how much does that mean, when Cartel inspectors make out the production reports?"

"So—?"

"So IC's using chandak the same way they've used mekronal—as a weapon against the Independents!" Terral hammered his palm with a bony fist. "Just look at the pattern. With mekronal, their crews can work in all atmospheres, set up bases at a hundredth the cost of anyone else, and claim satellite monopoly rights from the Federation on grounds of prior colonization."

Boone nodded slowly. "Yes. I know how that works."

"All right. That's straight commercial rivalry, so even though it cuts our throats we've got no comeback. But now comes Titan fever—a disease that kills men like flies when you treat it with any of the mill run of specifics. If you don't treat them—" Terral broke off, looked square at Boone. "Boone, do you know the story on that?"

"No, I'm afraid not."

"Then read this—a report from the top labs of your own damned organization. Don't ask me how I got it."

The Independents' rep was fumbling in a briefcase as he spoke. He drew out a thick blue-covered folder and handed it to Boone.

Boone stared down at it. *"Titan Fever: An investigation of Untreated Cases,"* the title read. The binder was stamped "MOST SECRET" in big block letters, and it bore the official seal of Interplanetary Cartel's central research unit.

But the thing that held his eye was the signature on the submission.

The signature of Martin Krobis.

Frowning, he riffled through the document to the final page:

"...In summary, then, the following tentative conclusions may be reported:

"1.   Although occasional deaths due to complications sometimes result from Titan fever, most untreated cases may be expected to recover.

"2.   However, there is definite evidence that such cases undergo an extreme mutation of the gametes.

"3. While no adverse physiological effects of this mutation are apparent in infants born to parents one or both of whom have been infected, significant mental changes and/or deterioration stand out clearly.

"4. No such mutative effect is evident in cases treated with chandak extract or their offspring.

"On the basis of available data, therefore, it is considered urgent that all cases of Titan fever developing among Interplanetary Cartel's personnel or their families be given prompt treatment with chandak extract.

"All base administrative chiefs are explicitly made responsible for seeing that such treatment is carried out as directed."

Stiff-fingered, Boone closed folder. Again, his eyes met Terral's.

The lean man's face had grown bleak as Mars' windswept deserts. "Do you know what it's going to mean when that report gets out?"

"I can imagine."

"Can you? I wonder." The other raised a clenched fist; shook it. "Boone, it means a Cartel-dominated solar system, the end of human freedom. IC's got a monopoly on chandak and they intend to hold it, Federation or no Federation. The rest of us won't have any choice but to come to them on their terms, or else gamble that our children will grow up gibbering idiots."

In spite of himself, Boone shuddered.

Terral kept on talking: "The production records tell the story. They say that Chandak's in short supply—so short that it comes in dribbles. But that report you read doesn't mention any shortage does it? All it gives is an order—flat directive to see that all IC's people are protected."

WEARILY, Boone nodded. "All right. You've sold me. Now tell me just how I fit in. What am I supposed to do?"

"Good!" The other slapped Boone's shoulder. "As to what you do, it's the same proposition that we talked about at Gandor City. The thing we're buying is your training. There's an Independent ship ramped in the main port, ready to grav-off. It's equipped for mekronal production. You take it out and find some Helgae."

Boone's heart leaped. "You mean—I break and run? I don't stand trial?"

"That's why we had Schilling get that release order."

The room seemed suddenly distorted. Boone paced the floor to hide his shaking.

He'd left Eileen on far Hyperion, a prisoner of the Helgae.

No, in spite of all Krobis' machinations, fate had thrown him a wild gambler's chance to reach her.

Terral's voice drummed at him: "That order cost us, Boone. Who cares, though, if it breaks the Cartel? Sure, you'll be a fugitive for awhile. But you'll be safe so long as nobody thinks to tie you in with us, and we can smooth the whole business over once we get our own source of mekronal and chandak…"

Pushing his jumbled thoughts aside, Boone pivoted. "What are we waiting for? Let's get started."

"Already?" Terral chuckled dryly. "Slow down. This is going to take a little doing." He bent over the desk, scribbled swiftly on a notepad, and then straightened. "Take this to the manager at Triangle Freight. Hot as you are, we're going to have to crate you up and send you out onto the ramp as cargo."

"Right." Boone slipped the scrawl into his pocket. "I'll be on my way, then."

"Good luck."

Boone answered with a wordless salute and, turning, strode from the office and the building.

He still felt a little dazed. How could it all have worked out so perfectly and so simply?

Only then, suddenly, a man appeared out of a doorway, hurrying in Boone's direction with head down—almost running.

Too late, Boone tried to sidestep. The man crashed into him and they both reeled, clinging to each other for support.

The next instant, hands gripped Boone from behind. A hard, unseen something rammed against his backbone. "Don't move, Boone!" clipped a tight, familiar voice.

Boone stiffened. "Krobis—!"

"Correct." The thing against Boone's back withdrew. Krobis stepped round into view, nerve-gun in hand, leaving his aides to hold the prisoner. His black eyes glittered. "For the record, you're under Cartel arrest again, in accordance with IC regulations."

Boone held his voice flat. "I can't stop you, Krobis. But when trial time comes, the Federation may not think much of this."

"You think not?" The Ganymedan base director smirked, and took a stand with too short legs wide-spraddled. "Personally, I'm more inclined to believe they'll cite me for a commendation—once they've heard my recording of your little talk with Terral."

For the fraction of a second, Boone stopped breathing. His lips were all at once so stiff he couldn't speak.

"That hit you, eh?" sneered Krobis. "You should have been more careful. All I was interested in to start was finding out who pressured through that release order for you. I didn't guess you had ties to the Independents, or that you planned to run out. But I'm glad you tried it. The recording makes your conviction certain, and puts us where we can jump the gun on Terral.

"Meanwhile, you stay where you belong—in IC's own Thelema guardhouse!"

CHAPTER FIVE

BOONE waited till the guard had left the cellblock to let in the group scheduled to conduct the preliminary inquiry. Then, with one last look out across the darkening ramp to where the Independent sphere-ship lay interned, he climbed onto the bunk, looped the end of the torn cloth noose up through the ventilator grating, twisted his collar still more awry, and stepped off into space.

The noose cut his neck, but not too badly. Most of his weight hung from the extra loop he'd run under his arms and round his chest. Yet the turned-up collar made it look like he was truly hanging by his neck alone.

There was a drone of voices from the hallway. Words drifted to him as the speakers paused outside the locked door.

"It's all set up," came the dipped tones of Martin Krobis. "We'll push through the special session of the board tonight, with a quick decision in favor of disciplinary discharge from Cartel service. The Federation court can hear the criminal case next cycle. By the end of the week he'll be on his way to Venus barracks."

Someone laughed raucously. A third voice crowed, "Leave it to Krobis!"

Then the bolt was snicking back, the block door opening. Quickly, Boone twisted his head to an appropriate angle. Closing his eyes, he let himself swing limp and motionless as he could.

The fraction of a second later one of the visitors choked, "Krobis! Look—"

"Damn him—!" This in tight fury from Krobis. "He can't cheat me this way. I won't let him!" Shoes slithered on the flooring. Quick! Help me!"

Hands lifted Boone. A knife hacked at the cloth noose.

The fabric ripped through at last. Still limp of limb, head lolling, Boone let himself be lowered to the bunk.

Then Krobis' voice rang close beside him: "This noose—! There's something funny—"

Stubby fingers tugged apart the double loops.

Boone slumped sidewise, away from Krobis, so that the other was strained far forward and off balance.

Then, in one swift, convulsive movement, he drove his elbow deep into his enemy's unprotected midriff.

The wind went out of the base director's lungs in a gust. He bent double...hung tottering, face shock-contorted.

Twisting, Boone whipped his hand up...chopped down with all his might on the back of Krobis' neck.

Krobis slammed forward on his face on the floor.

As he landed, the spell of startlement that had held the others broke. With an incoherent roar, the man at the left lunged forward.

Boone jerked back. Writhing, flat on the bunk, he jackknifed his legs up and lashed out with both feet, straight at his attacker's face.

The man tried to dodge. Barely, in time, his head flicked aside.

But it was too late for him to twist his shoulders.

There was the brittle *crack* of a collarbone snapping. The man catapulted back, clear across the cellblock.

But now the third man was upon Boone, swinging a nerve-gun. The guard crowded close behind him.

Before Boone could move, the barrel gashed open his forehead. A fist hammered at his temple. The guard clawed at him...crushed his flailing legs in a mighty bear hug.

Spasmodically, Boone clutched the nerve-gun; jammed it upward.

A grunt of pain echoed as a trigger-guard wrenched a forefinger. The man who held the weapon reared back sharply and let go of it.

Boone backhanded the butt, striking for the man's Adam's

apple.

The blow hit home. Choking, Boone's assailant tried to break free, tripped, and pitched backwards to the floor.

Boone spun the gun, reversed it, blazed a charge at the guard, dangerously close to his own legs.

The burly jailer gave a single paroxysmic jerk, then crumpled.

Blood from the barrel-gash spilling into his eyes, Boone lurched up and lunged for the open doorway.

Someone clutched at his ankle. Kicking free, not even turning, he charged on into the corridor and broke for the building exit—half-running, half-staggering.

Then the last door was swinging shut behind him. He plunged into the shadows along a warehouse.

Behind him, chaos and rising voices. A com-box blared, "All guards alert! Escape! This prisoner's dangerous! Don't let him get off the ramp! All guards alert...!"

Forspark lights flared at the gates. Somewhere a surface carrier rumbled into clattering motion.

BOONE sagged back against the warehouse and swabbed the blood from his eyes. Then, still breathing hard, running almost doubled, he raced not towards the gates, but away from them, towards the black block that was the airlock power station.

Shadows again, and another pause for breath. Sirens blasting. The rumble of more carriers.

In spite of his tension, Boone smiled thinly. Swinging round, he moved warily on towards the station entrance.

The two men on duty stood in the doorway, peering out across the ramp.

Back flat to the wall, Boone silently edged towards them...closer...closer...

One said, "What's that—?" and started to turn.

Boone leaped forward, triggering a beam from the nerve-gun.

The two duty men went down as one. Dragging them inside,

Boone kicked the door shut, then turned to the lock control equipment. In seconds, he had levered out the gear that prevented the outer locks from opening till the inner were closed and sealed.

Crossing to the emergency control bank, then, he threw the first switch.

Heavy-duty motors spun to droning life. A red light flashed on the board.

Ten seconds later the red light clicked off. A green light blazed in its stead, and the motors cut off.

The inner locks were open!

Dry-lipped, Boone threw the second switch.

Motors. Red light. Green light. Silence.

Or almost silence. For now a whistling sound came dimly, apparent even within the building.

The sound of the ramp-bubble's precious atmosphere escaping!

Swinging up a heavy beryllium wrench, Boone smashed the switches.

That made his gamble good for fifteen minutes leeway…a quarter of an hour at least that the locks would stay jammed open.

Boone threw down the wrench. Then, pivoting, he strode to the door and jerked it open.

On all sides, in the distance, men were running, shouting. There was a low roar of atmosphere compressors, trying to compensate for the changing pressure. Now sirens blasted.

While he watched, a surface carrier skidded around a warehouse and hurtled towards the airlock power station.

Ice-nerved, Boone waited, weapon ready.

The carrier screamed to a stop beside the door. Men leaped down.

Boone stepped from the shadows, swung his nerve-gun. "Back, damn you!"

The men froze, staring.

Vaulting aboard the vehicle, Boone jammed the gun against

the back of the driver's neck. "We're going onto the ramp-out to that Independent ship."

Wordless, the man pressed buttons, swung the steering lever. The carrier jerked forward.

More dragging seconds. The great sphere on the ramp looming ever larger.

Boone clipped, "Pull in beside the lift-shaft!"

The driver obeyed.

Stunning him with a beam-edge, Boone jumped down, gun concealed once more, as a uniformed Federation trooper stepped from the lift. He made his voice harsh, peremptory: "Who's in charge here?"

It brought the trooper up short. "Sergeant Martov, sir."

"The crew's aboard?"

"Yes, sir. Security ordered them interned on the ship so word wouldn't get out that we'd taken over."

"Then take me to the sergeant. Fast!"

"Yes, sir." The man spun about.

Boone waited till they were both inside the lift, then hit the other behind the ear with the nerve-gun's barrel.

The trooper went down, unconscious.

ROLLING him out of the shaft, onto the ramp, Boone shoved the lift control lever to the fifth stop, the crew quarters.

The lift ground upwards.

There was another trooper on duty on the fifth level exit. Boone paralyzed him with the nerve-gun, not even speaking, and ran on down the corridor to the wardroom.

Two Independent ensigns sat playing N'rlan with a navigator. One glanced up as Boone burst in; he half-rose, mouth gaping. "My God! The mek-man!"

Boone's heart leaped. "Then you know about me?"

"Of course." This from the other ensign. "Terral had the whole ship readied to take off on two minutes' notice. Only then they grabbed you, and the damn Cartel nailed us down here with a secret internment order from the Federation."

"But you still could make a run? Everything's aboard and ready?"

"Sure, if the locks would only open. There's just a sergeant and three troopers on duty."

Triumph surged through Boone—a wild, raw-nerved elation that left his sagging back against the doorframe, dizzy.

In a voice that didn't even remotely resemble his own, he said, "The locks are open."

The others took over, after that. As from afar, Boone heard the terse commands, the bellowed orders.

Then lights were flashing, hatches slamming. There was the grav-off's momentary lurch and wallow; the swift rush up, the hiss of passage through the airlocks while the sphere rocked like a cork in the vortex of the bubble's escaping atmosphere.

By the time the medmen had sealed the gash in his forehead, the ship was hurtling out across the void on its appointed course, away from Mars, towards far Hyperion.

Hyperion, and Eileen Rey.

Though there was little enough time for Boone to think about her.

And perhaps that was best, also. For the memory of her was with him every moment, like a shadow, and when he paused even for a second, dark fantasies rose and his belly knotted.

So he was glad when the Independents' wizened, thong-tough captain called him in for consultation in the chartroom.

The hurtling heavens flashed on the wall-screen, sharp-focussed by the microreel projector. The captain raised a long light-pointer. "This is our track. To save time, we'll cut short through The Belt and Jupiter's orbit. It's dangerous, but it may fool them."

A chill touched Boone. "You think they'll follow?"

"After what you did—those crippled airlocks?" The captain's laugh was curt and mirthless. "They'll have the whole Federation fleet out hunting for us. The only chance we've got is to find cover."

"And even if we do, we'll still be outlawed?"

"That's right." The captain shrugged. "So far as I'm concerned, I might as well tear up my ticket."

"But if we get mekronal and chandak—"

"That's why I chanced it."

Boone's backbone prickled. He stared at the screen in aching silence.

Overhead, the com-box crackled: "Detector room reporting. We are getting blips off Ceres."

"The asteroid station," the captain muttered. He turned to Boone. "You may as well know: I doubt we'll make it. Because the Cartel ships will hunt us, right along with the Federation fleet. The Europa units, Ganymede, Callisto—they'll all be out. With that many ships, they can set up a screen and follow us on their detectors. Even though we sneak through, they'll still track us and close in as soon as we grav down."

Boone remained tensely silent.

Now the microreel image showed Saturn rising.

Saturn, mother planet of bleak Titan.

Somewhere in the shadow of those vast, shimmering rings Hyperion, too, moved in its orbit.

Hyperion: Another potential source of the precious mekronal and chandak. Another world of strange domed Helgae cities.

Only Hyperion was turning out to be a trap, not refuge. With Cartel and Federation ships alike spread out in a filter-screen across the void, there'd be no chance for this lone Independent ship to land or hide there.

Unless—

BOONE all at once was rigid. "Captain," he asked, "could you run to Uranus?"

"Uranus—!" The wizened officer swung, stared at him. "Are you crazy, man? Why would anyone in his right mind want to go there?"

"That's not the question. Could you make it?"

The other's eyes narrowed. "Yes. I suppose so."

"And could you think up a reason for it—some excuse that the Fedfleet might find convincing?"

"Maybe."

Boone drew in a breath. "Then start getting your story together." He strode to the screen, traced a course with his finger. "If you arc it right, we'll pass through Hyperion's field of attraction. When that happens, you can shoot a handful of us down in carriers without even stopping. You'll take the ship on towards Uranus. The Federation, the Cartel, won't even know we've left you."

The captain rocked. "Boone, you *are* crazy!"

"No!" As if by magic, the chill had left Boone. He burned with sudden, feverish excitement. "The only trick will be to breach the ice-shell. For that, you can rig an unmanned carrier or two with warheads. They'll blast a hole. The rest of the party can go down through it."

"But why?" the captain spluttered. "Why Hyperion, of all places? I've come this far because my orders from Terral were to do exactly what you wanted. But this—this gibberish about an ice-shell—"

"—Isn't gibberish!" Boone finished for him fiercely. "You thought this was to be a prospecting expedition, Captain. But that's not so, not really. Because I've been down on Hyperion before and underneath the surface ice is a warm world with at least one big Helgae city! All we have to do is set up a base, start processing mekronal, and claim the whole satellite for Associated Independents."

The captain's eyes distended. "Boone, do you mean it?"

"Of course I mean it. I was aboard a sphere that crashed after monsters hit it. That's why we've got to work fast. Martin Krobis knows about it. Unless we hurry, the Cartel may beat us to it with a unit."

But the captain was no longer listening. Face flushed, brow furrowed, he was studying the microreel-projected wall-chart. "I can pass the word to headquarters to send out a sphere-load of equipment. And I've got enough mekronal aboard to give maybe half-a-dozen men protection without a bubble; Terral bribed some Cartel hand to steal a little for him..."

He swung to the com-box, then snapped orders.

The quiet of the chart room dissolved into seething bedlam.

While Boone stood by, warheads were fitted to two carriers. With five mekronal-treated men, he crowded aboard a third.

Then, on the visiscreen, bleak Hyperion was looming. Boone waited, taut and strain-straught, hand on the carrier-release lever.

Now, slowly, the mountain peaks so far away began to form a pattern...a distortion and projection of the same pattern Boone had seen before, looking up at the crags that pierced the ice-shell. For a moment he almost thought that in a prick of black he was seeing the rift made by the fallen Cartel sphere-ship.

Not that it mattered; enough that he had a mark to shoot at.

The captain's voice rasped from the com-box: "Boone. You'd better hurry. Our detectors show Federation ships approaching."

THE last lingering fragments of Boone's hesitation vanished. He pressed the button set to trigger the first carrier.

Like a scarlet lance, the sleek craft shot from its cradle—speeding out from the sphere; hurtling down towards the ice-shell, faster and faster.

Boone pressed the second button.

Another explosive-laden carrier speared through the void upon its mission.

Boone turned in his seat. "Hatches—?"

"Secured and sealed," a brawny, blond-haired giant behind him grunted.

For the fraction of a second Boone stared at the rocky face, the grim-set jaw.

The others, too: four stone-featured crewmen, each waiting in silence despite the tension.

A tightness came to Boone's throat.

Only then, once again, the sphere-ship captain's voice was rasping: "Boone, those blips are coming closer."

Tight-lipped, Boone pressed the third button...the button that triggered this final carrier.

He jarred back, then, as the pressure of the craft's swift acceleration hit him.

But it only lasted for a moment. Free of the sphere-ship, the carrier sped out into space along the path slashed by the two before it. Behind it, the hurtling mother-globe was already fading, as it raced on across Saturn's orbit towards Uranus.

Down, down the carriers lanced, straight for Hyperion's ice-masked surface...closer and closer, faster and faster.

Then, while Boone held his breath, the first struck.

A flash of fire, a vast exploding cataclysm. Ice spraying out like splattering water...

Before the cloud of icy splinters could even settle, the second carrier crashed home. New jets of spray leaped skyward. Great cracks appeared, from here a tracery of fine, shimmering lines against the satellite's frigid surface.

Boone slowed the third carrier till it hung almost motionless. Taut-nerved, he waited.

Slowly, the drifting blast-cloud cleared. A pit yawned in the ice.

With wary patience, Boone dropped the carrier closer to the surface...hovered momentarily above the pit edge.

Color flashed in the depths—the color of flower-fields, of verdure.

Of a sudden the jagged ice-claws didn't matter. Boone zoomed the carrier in a great loop, then dived it back again straight for the pit, the color.

Death's own tension rode with them. Once Boone thought he could hear the echo of a choked off prayer.

Then the pit's ice walls were closing around them. The target below seemed so very tiny...

The carrier struck ice, an out-thrust fragment. A shudder ran through its strain-racked structure. Veering, it crashed into the razor shards along the lower lip of the hole.

The impact flung Boone savagely against his belt. His head snapped back so hard that for a moment he thought his neck was broken. Behind him, through the scream of torn and tortured metal, a man shouted shrilly.

Then the carrier was falling. Barely in time, Boone caught the globe control and spun it.

END for end, the carrier flipped over in the air. Swinging like a pendulum by its nose, it settled to earth with a jarring shock that would have torn the ramping fins from a craft less sturdy.

Boone sagged in his seat. Then, rallying, he peered upward.

Ice still was falling. Apparently the force of the carrier's down-thrust—coupled with the earlier blasts—had shaled off great chunks of the ice-shell's undersurface.

As for the ship, the others—Boone loosed his belt; scrambled round to see.

The blond giant already was bending over another crewman.

Boone stiffened. "Is it bad?"

The other straightened, shook his head. "I don't think so. He's just out cold; I think he hit his head on something."

"Good." Boone breathed again. "I think I'll chance an all-clear to the sphere-ship."

Turning to the visiscreen, he twisted dials, pressed buttons. Dimly at first, the mother craft appeared, far out in space.

Only then, while he watched, another sphere swept across the shining panel, followed by yet another and another.

Cartel ships.

There could be no escape from them. Not when they rallied in such numbers.

Even in that moment, the Independent ship was slowly, swinging.

A numb sickness came to Boone. He'd counted on days alone here...days to lay waste the Helgae city till at last he found Eileen.

Now that margin was reduced to cycles. For once Krobis found that he—Boone—and three carriers were missing from the sphere-ship just after it left Hyperion's orbit, it would be mere hours before Cartel ships were landing.

After that, there'd be Venus Barracks, as well as the emptiness of failure.

If he could only find Eileen before it happened...

He flicked off the visiscreen's main switch.

Like the hideous magnification of an echo, a scream rang through the carrier.

Boone whirled.

As he did so, the blond giant's head appeared, framed in the power converter hatchway. His eyes were white-rimmed, staring, his left arm limp and bloody.

"Monsters!" he shrieked. "Monsters—!"

Those were the last words that he ever spoke. For as he shouted, six great clawed hands stretched through the hatch behind him and convulsed around his body.

The two top ones tore his head off...

CHAPTER SIX

BOONE died a thousand times in that one moment. Then, shouting a warning to the four remaining crewmen, he caught up an axe from the rack of emergency equipment and crept towards converter-room and monster.

The thing had withdrawn now, dragging the dead man's body with it—for what awful purpose Boone could not even guess.

Yet the question that lay implicit in the thought made him pause just short of the door for the fraction of a second. It turned out to be a pause that saved his life.

For in that same instant a claw-hand snaked back through the hatchway. Filth-encrusted nails scraped along his arm, endeavoring to seize him.

Boone jerked back with a hoarse, involuntary oath. Wildly, he swung the axe.

The keen blade bit into the monster's extended arm. A muddy sludge of blood gushed forth. The claw-hand jerked back.

Yet the thing made no sound—not a single groan or snarl or murmur.

Boone hesitated, even more wary than before. He kicked a fallen spanner towards the doorway.

Like lightning, the monster lunged from its hideout—and now Boone saw why it had made no outcry.

The thing had no head! It consisted of arms only—six hairy, humanoid arms radiating out from a central core that looked like an enormous mushroom button.

Careening, the creature changed course. The arms clawed out to clutch Boone.

Leaping wide, he slashed with the axe—a savage blow with all his strength behind it, straight for the central core, the button.

There was a sound like a watermelon bursting. The button

broke and flew apart, not so much sliced as shattered. A sickening stench erupted through the cabin. The arms sagged, limp save for spasmodic twitchings.

Half-sick with the sight, the smell, Boone stumbled back.

But before he could even drop the axe, a new cry came.

It rose behind him, this time—from the cabin's other end, the hatchway to the landing ladder.

Boone spun, ran towards the ladder.

From the bottom of the narrow shaft, a white-faced crewman beckoned in a frenzy. "Out—! Get out!" He vanished through the exit port.

Boone dropped the axe and, sliding, plummeted down the ladder. In seconds he, too, was stumbling through the port.

The crewman who'd shouted crouched on the ground in the shadow of the ramping fins beside one of his fellows, the man who'd lain unconscious since they landed. "Look!" His whole arm shook as he pointed.

Boone veered, then froze.

If what had gone before was nightmare, surely this was utter madness. For from beyond the circling hills, a hand was stretching towards them—a hand vast beyond all human concept! Like living columns carved in flesh, the fingers reached out, nails glittering in the filtered sunlight of the ice-shell.

With a mighty effort, Boone forced himself to motion. Lunging back through the port, he tore a long-range blaster from its wall-clip, then leaped to the ground once more and raced away, off to one side where there was space clear of the ship for him to use the weapon.

His action seemed to break the paralysis of the crouching crewman. Jumping up, the fellow disappeared for a moment into the carrier, then rushed out again with a second blaster and darted after Boone.

The giant hand's shadow fell upon the ship. The circling fingers closed about it. Boone stumbled to a halt. Twisting, he swung round the blaster…triggered a bolt at the clutching hand.

For the barest instant the hand stopped short. Then, in one savage, spasmodic motion, the great fingers clamped down on the carrier, clenching.

THERE was a clash and crash of rending metal, a roar of compressor tanks exploding. Flame spurted out between the crushing fingers.

Wrist muscles bulging, the hand whipped high into the air, then down again with earth-shaking force. The fingers opened...spilled out the crumpled mass of wreckage that had been the ship.

...Wreckage, and the pitiful, broken bodies of the two crewmen who had been trapped inside.

A hoarse cry burst from the throat of their comrade, the man who'd followed Boone. Whipping up his blaster, he blazed bolt after bolt into the hand.

As a human might slap at a mosquito, the hand smashed down and crushed him, then started towards Boone.

Shock-rocked, quaking, he dived into the closest flower clump's cover...rolled and writhed through the foliage, flat against the earth.

Overhead the hand paused, searching.

Then, bare yards from him, suddenly, it fell.

But not in a blow. No. This was different. For it fell limp and sagging, as if the muscles all at once had lost their power.

Boone lay like a statue—frozen, waiting.

Nothing happened.

The tension in him grew moment by moment, till he could hold it down no longer. He surged to his feet, blaster at the ready.

But the hand did not move. Before his eyes, as he stood there, it was...melting...oozing away into the ground in stinking rivulets of slime.

Numbly, Boone moved along it; and now, incredibly, he could see its termination, just below the rim of the nearest hills.

For it was an arm without a body—an arm that trailed off into nothing, like a figure cast in wax.

Yet there too lay the carrier, crushed and crumpled...the broken bodies of the men.

This limp, dead arm had done that...

It was more than human mind could take. Boone slumped to the ground and cowered there, shaking.

Nor would the seizure pass. It was as if he suddenly were chilling. Cold crept through his veins in icy tendrils to the very marrow of his bones.

Harder and harder he shook. Yet still no surcease came. His whole body was aching now and it dawned upon him, dimly, that no shock alone could leave him thus yet still alive.

Then, at long last, the chills and cold departed, driven out by a quick, fierce heat. His mouth grew dry. His tongue took on new thickness. Flowers, hills, wreckage—all seemed distorted. He burned as with a flaming fever...

Fever—?

He knew, then.

Titan fever!

What else could it be, here on Hyperion, but that strange pyrexia that mutated Man's gametes?

So there was no hope for him, no answer...

He never knew for sure what happened after that—how much was reality, how much fever-madness.

For delirium came, and in that state he wandered. The hills rolled down in lowering barriers of menace, and flowers talked to him, and he walked beside strange streams.

And then, sometimes, it seemed that Eileen stood beside him...that he could hear her rippling laughter echo, and taste her lips, and smell the fragrance of her hair.

But Eileen was still a prisoner of the Helgae, sealed in a sphere somewhere within their weird, domed cities.

That meant he had to find her.

So he wandered on, babbling of mekronal and chandak...precious chandak, the only remedy that could save him from his fate.

And Krobis was there, too, and Terral—all the others. Sometimes they mocked; sometimes they helped him.

Not that it mattered. For now, an at once, he could get away from his own body, floating cloud-like in space beneath three great green suns.

The monsters came, then.

THE first was in the image of the Helgae—lumpish, mottled, but with a yawning orifice that he knew somehow was meant to be a mouth. Twice it tried to swallow him as he floated, then faded away again when he rolled away beyond its reach.

The second took the appearance of his own father. Its face pressed close, all clipped mustache and burning eyes and shiny skin.

He shrank before it.

But the face kept following him, pressing closer, and the feeling grew within him that if the tight gray lips should ever open, he would surely die. So he surged away in utter ter-ror...fled through the green-tinged sky-sea around him.

But his muscles were all at once like water, his movements as inadequate and slow as only the responses in a dream can be.

Desperately, he tried to move faster...faster...

The face rushed in. He screamed aloud.

Then he was falling. Head over heels, he pitched down into depths at once black as night and shining white and shimmering with weird iridescence.

The third monster rose out of the mists beneath him.

It was a thing of horror beyond the telling, with a body Boone sensed more than he saw.

But from that body rose a long and sinuously slender eyestalk, surmounted with a huge human eye.

It was the eye that held Boone; for as he stared into it in mute, numb fascination, he knew that it would draw him ever closer till at last the slime-mass that was the body could swirl out and suck him in.

A black wave of despair engulfed him. Of a sudden his

palms, his whole body, were drenched with sweat. The feeling that he was falling faded. Vaguely, he became aware of roughnesses beneath him. A breeze washed over him and he chilled.

Slowly, painfully, he opened his eyes...stared up into the murk of night.

But it was a night that was already dying. Far off to one side, a dim glow marked the coming of the day.

Cords of tension fell away. Once again, at last, he lived in a world of reality, not nightmare.

He hugged it to him; drew in the chill security of it with gusty, lung-expanding breaths.

The gray glow in the distance spread. Weakly, he sat up to look about him—and stared instead into the pale malevolence of a great, baleful, swaying eye!

He froze, not daring to move or speak.

For the thing before him was the monster of his fever-madness—the eyestalked horror from the dream.

Yet he knew—*he knew!*—that he had left delirium's valley. This was reality! Without question, the fever had waned and gone.

Then what—?

He had no answer. Not here, not now. He could only wait, and hope, and perhaps pray.

But while he watched, not daring to so much as flick an eye or move a muscle, the thing before him began to eddy slowly closer.

New sweat rolled down Boone's spine. A knot of tension drew tight within his belly.

Sinuously, the monster's eyestalk swayed. The huge orb atop stared at Boone unblinking.

Stiff-fingered, too fear-straught to even look away, he slid his hands out in arcs along the ground.

But they touched no stick, no stone, no clod, no debris. He remained as he had been, a warrior sore beset, without a weapon.

And still the monster eddied closer...

He could not even break and run. Weak as he was, he dared not even trust his muscles.

Spasmodically, his nails scraped at the dirt.

The dirt—!

He dug his fingers deep into it...sucked a ragged breath to ease his hammering heart.

Like a serpent poising to strike, the monster paused. The horror that was its body drew together.

With a wild shout, Boone hurled the dirt square into the glaring eye.

THE eyestalk whipped back, quivering and pulsing. Then, in an instant, recovering, the creature spilled forward in a rush.

But already Boone was twisting, scrambling, clawing his way along the ground.

Then there was a rock beneath his hands, big as a man's head. In spite of his weakness he clutched it, swung it up.

The monster swept down upon him as he pivoted.

Boone hurled the rock.

It struck at the base of the weird thing's eyestalk. With a snapping sound, the orb's stem broke.

Twitching, writhing, the body halted. Then, as with the giant arm, the other monsters, the creature's whole structure began to shrivel and ooze away in slime.

Panting, shaking, Boone slumped back to the ground, his brain a cauldron bubbling with inchoate thoughts.

Like a mosaic, then, the pieces fell into place.

This whole void-area—and this area only—seemed to crawl with mad phantasms...lunatic life forms like none that Man had ever seen before. Out of nowhere, they materialized aboard the Cartel's sphere-ships. Here, on Hyperion; Titan, too.

Those were the facts. Now, suddenly, they took on form and pattern.

For in his delirium, Boone knew he'd had nightmares of this specific slime-drenched horror.

Awakening, his fever gone, he'd faced the hideous thing on reality's plane.

And the Helgae could play strange tricks with human minds...

The Helgae—they were the correlating factor!

The Cartel had come and raped their silent cities for the sake of mekronal and chandak.

So lacking the power of discourse, words to protest, they'd struck back in their own dark way.

Somehow, they'd reached into men's deep subconscious and dredged up monsters—the paranoid delusions of fevered brains.

Then, as the mediums of another day had claimed to give spirits ectoplasmic body, so now the Helgae materialized nightmares into life!

What armor could turn aside such a weapon?

Yet beyond it lay the threat of Titan fever. For that, too, could be a blow struck by the Helgae—the main attack, designed to cripple the mass-mind of the whole, far-flung human race.

Boone shuddered.

Yet strength rose in him, not despair. For with knowledge, the fears he'd felt of the unknown vanished. He looked about in the growing light with new, fresh eyes.

The landscape had changed from that which he last remembered. This ground lay in altogether different contours.

Frowning, he turned.

Now, with a shock, he found himself staring out on a familiar scene: the arcs and domes and bubbles of the self-same sprawling Helgae city where he and Eileen had lain entombed.

...Where Eileen still might lie.

It was a thought to make his belly churn, his heart pound, wrenching cruelly at every atom of his being. He sagged, gripped his head between his hands."

THE sleeve of his shirt fell across his face, ripped wide. Incredulously, he discovered that everything he wore hung in rags and tatters. Even his shoes were slashed and mud-caked.

How far had he strayed in his fever-wanderings? How long had it been since delirium struck?

He ran his fingers over cheek and chin: a three days' growth of beard at least…maybe more.

Not that it mattered. For he was alive; and out of horror, hypothesis had been born. If, truly, the materializing monsters and Titan fever were weapons of the beleaguered Helgae, then a truce must somehow be arranged, even if it meant complete human withdrawal from all satellites of Saturn.

That called for action by the Federation: action that the Cartel's chiefs would fight with tooth and nail.

Yet IC might well defeat itself by its own opposition. All apart from any Helgae menace, the Independents would rally instantly to whatever cause should threaten to disrupt the Cartel's mekronal production.

But that could wait; Eileen could not. Here, now, somehow, he had to save her.

Or was that hopeless?

Only time and fate could give the answers. Meanwhile, the least that he could do was try.

Unsteadily, Boone rose. He cursed the fever that had drained his strength.

It was then he heard the crashing blaster bolt beyond the ridge, off to his right, away from the Helgae city.

Again, his heart leaped. Blasters spoke for men, not Helgae—human help, here on Hyperion with him.

Lurching, stumbling, he dragged himself up the hill.

At last, the crest.

Below, the hull of a ramped Independent carrier, scarlet and silver, came into view.

Now strength surged through Boone. He broke into a staggering run, straight down the slope.

Only then, as he careened too fast past a brushy thicket, something thrust out between his flying feet. He spilled forward in a bruising, sliding fall.

A voice rasped, "Don't move! I've got you covered!"

Painfully, Boone twisted.

A man stood in the shadow of the thicket—a man with a blaster, a man who wore the blue-gray field outfit of an Interplanetary Cartels guard.

The other's lean face split in a mirthless grin as he stalked forward. "You're Boone, aren't you?" And then: "Krobis had you figured. He said you'd come in if you spotted an Independent ship."

"Krobis—?" Boone's lips went stiff. "You mean, he's here?"

"Of course he's here." The guard chuckled. "You told him about this Helgae city underneath the ice-shell yourself, didn't you? So he set up a base but pronto, with manpower enough to fight off monsters. He plans to start blasting the domes before next cycle, get a mekronal unit into production, and claim Hyperion for the next Cartel."

He broke off, gestured to Boone with the blaster. "Get up! We're going in. The way Krobis feels about you, catching you is good for Earth-leave and a sergeant's rating."

NUMBLY, Boone heaved himself to his feet, stood swaying.

Was this to be the end of all his sufferings—back where he started, a prisoner en route to a cell in Venus Barracks? Was the Cartel to go on butchering the Helgae until opposing life forms clashed in full-scale war?

Above all, was he never to know the truth as to Eileen's fate? Did this mark the end of his last dim chance to save her?

For all illusion had died in him. Whatever else might be, there was no mercy in Martin Krobis. Ego, vengeance, ambition—those were the man's three key dynamics. Nothing else mattered to him; not truth, nor justice, nor even the life of Eileen Rey. He'd laugh at theories...gloat over his triumphs...sacrifice the rest of the human race if need be for the sake of the Cartel and his own fame and power.

"Get moving," the guard clipped. "We're going in."

Wearily, Boone turned and stumbled down the slope through

the brush towards the ramped carrier.

But for all despair, fatigue, a spark still burned within him.

Krobis must not win! He must not!

Ahead, the ground fell away more sharply; and there were trees and bushes, saplings.

With cold deliberation, Boone tripped—pitched forward—and let himself fall headlong.

But as he fell, he caught the limb of a slender treelet.

It bent almost double.

Prone now, Boone clung to it.

The guard ran to him, blaster ready. "Get up, you!" Face a mask of wary menace, he stepped closer.

Too close.

Boone let go of the limb.

The treelet snapped back. Branches slashed into the guard's face.

Out of reserves he had not known existed, Boone drew strength to hurl himself into spasmodic action. He twisted, kicked for the guard's legs with all his might.

The man went down with a hoarse, choked shout.

Boone lurched down upon him. His elbow smashed at the other's temple.

The guard sagged, glaze-eyed and groggy.

Snatching up the blaster, Boone hit his adversary with the butt, a savage blow.

The guard went limp, unconscious.

Sick, sobbing for breath, Boone slumped beside him.

But only for a moment.

Then, rallying, he fumbled the rations from the other's belt-case, gulping down the concentrates in great, gagging, half-chewed bites.

His protesting stomach writhed. For long seconds he thought he was going to vomit.

But that, too, passed. The sugars, the ectoids, began to reach his bloodstream.

Strength came with them.

Tight-lipped, clutching the blaster, Boone began the long, weary climb back up the hill.

...Back, and beyond, to the strange, domed city of the Helgae...and to Eileen Rey...

CHAPTER SEVEN

HE saw the light-shafts first—two glowing cones of color that speared down from a single halo-source high in this vastest of all the bubble chambers. The beam on the left shone rich with hues of deepest purple. The other, the one on the right, shimmered golden as Earth's September sun.

Numb, wordless, Boone moved forward with unsteady steps.

Now he saw the cones' bases as well as source; and all at once his heart was pounding, pounding, till he thought that it must surely burst.

For each light played on a separate transparent sphere that floated, somehow invisibly suspended, at eye level in the bubble-room.

A nude human body lay within each sphere.

Shaking, Boone made his way to the gold-bathed globe.

But the figure inside was that of a man, a stranger, with a calm, vaguely familiar face.

Boone turned to the second sphere, that on which played the cone of purple light.

This time, he looked upon a woman.

Eileen!

He swayed, still not daring to allow himself to believe it.

How had he found her in this weird maze, this bubble-catacomb? How long had he wandered through dim-lit passageways and domed, echoing chambers? How many times had he despaired?

It was as if destiny had walked beside him, guiding.

Destiny, or…other minds. Alien minds, perhaps greater than his.

But whatever the answer, he'd kept on, and he'd found her. That was what counted.

Now, while he watched, new radiance suffused the chamber.

The light cones dimmed; and as they faded, the spheres floated slowly, gently, to the floor.

Then, as on that other, dreamlike day that seemed so long ago, there was a crash of silent thunder. The globes split, fell apart.

Boone dropped to one knee. With trembling fingers he touched Eileen's bare breast.

Her flesh was warm, her heart beat steady. Like a child awakening, her lashes fluttered. Then, lids already lifting, she turned and looked up at him with calm, untroubled eyes.

A sob rose in Boone's throat. He pressed her to him.

She laughed, ever so softly; and tenderness was in it. Cool fingers smoothed his brow, his hair. "Fred, you sound so—worried..."

His words came in a jumble, then: "You—you're all right? There's—nothing's happened?"

"No, of course not." She sounded not even quite certain of his meaning. "I only went to sleep for a little while; that's all."

The last tension drained from Boone's taut body. Weak, tremulous, unsteady, he slumped beside her amid the segments of the shattered sphere. "There's been so much, so many things—" He groped for words.

Only then, before he could say more, a distant impact rocked the chamber.

The impact of a demolition charge exploding.

In spite of emotional drain, exhaustion, Boone went rigid. "Krobis!"

"What—?" Eileen's blue eyes distended. "Fred, you mean he's here?"

"Yes, with plans for blasting apart this whole cursed Helgae city." Boone stumbled erect. "Quick! We've got to go!"

THE girl rose beside him, then looked down in sudden, swift abashment. A flush swept up her throat. Her face turned scarlet. "My clothes—where are they?"

A man's voice answered, "Here."

As one, Boone and Eileen spun around.

The stranger, he who had lain in the golden sphere, was getting up. Calmly, he strode to a low ledge on the far side of the bubble and picked up one of two bulky bundles; tossed it deftly to Eileen. "Everything is there."

Boone gripped his blaster. He moved a quick step forward. "You! Who are you?"

"They call me Lor."

"A name's no answer. Where'd you come from? How'd you get here?"

The other bent to pick up the second bundle, then straightened and, turning, stood full-face to Boone. "You...do not know? You cannot guess?"

Boone studied him, staring narrow-eyed at the calm, strangely familiar face. A youthful face, yet with eyes somehow old beyond all years.

A prickling ran up and down Boone's spine. "You—look—like me!"

"Of course." Lor smiled, turned to Eileen. "Surely you can tell?"

Her hand rose to her throat. Her face grew pale. "I—I don't know. You're like Fred...or—or—my father—"

"Yes." The sphere-man nodded gravely. "Indeed, I am—can only be—like both of you."

The silence echoed, then.

But it was a silence too taut to last for long. It had to break.

"You—can only be—like us?" Boone forced out the words.

Again, the other nodded. "Yes." And then: "Because—I am your son..."

Somewhere too close, another demolition charge exploded. But for Boone, the room rocked more with the stranger's words than from the blast.

"No!" he choked. "No!" Beside him, Eileen had slumped dazed-faced to the floor.

The sphere-man sighed. "I know. They told me it would be hard for you to understand."

"They—?"

"The ones you call the Helgae." For the first time, emotion seemed to grip Lor. He stared down at the bulky bundle in his hands; then, opening it, spread out an array of Cartel crewman's clothes. "They are an old race, older than you can know; and wise. They wanted no war with anyone, but there was no way for them to speak to a life form so unlike theirs. So, when your ships attacked their cities on the world called Titan, they drew monsters from your minds to slow your onslaughts, then sought some way to bridge the barrier between your different brains."

Boone caught his breath. "You mean—mutation—?"

"It was the only answer." The man who claimed him father bent to slide on shoes. "By casting their powers of mind in human bodies through the contagion you call Titan fever, the source of conflict between your separate species once and for all could be removed."

"Of course!" All of a sudden Boone was pacing. "Only then, our sphere-ship hit Hyperion, broke the ice-shell—"

"—And menaced another whole Helgae world." Lor shrugged into a jacket. "It made the danger too great for them to wait on normal human reproduction and maturing.

"But you two were on that sphere-ship—and you were male and female, man and woman."

"Then—that's why they trapped us!"

"Yes. While you lay in your sphere here, in the state you call unconscious, your seed was planted in the woman. When growth began, the egg itself was taken, processed. By science beyond your human dreams, they speeded the whole cycle of gestation, then brought me on to manhood in days instead of years. The mind-rays drained all knowledge from both of you, gave it to me, that I might be able properly to play my role."

Boone stopped short in his pacing. "Your role—?"

"You'd call it that." Now fully dressed, the other straightened. "I am a messenger, a human spokesman for the Helgae, with no other goal than to help our race live at peace."

"There'll be men who take convincing of that."

"You mean—men like the one named Martin Krobis?"

Boone stared. "Krobis—? You know about him?"

"Of course." His mutant son still smiled. "The mind-rays poured your every thought into me—even those too utterly alien for the Helgae themselves to understand. So, I know of Krobis: the things he's done; the way he thinks; the fact that he is here now, blasting at this very city—"

Like an exclamation point, new impact came. Thread-like cracks shot through the radiance of the bubble chamber's inner surface. The floor shook till Boone could hardly stand.

LOR'S face went grim. His voice rang with sudden tension: "Come, quickly. We dare not die in this mad destruction. We dare not!"

He pivoted as he spoke, moved swiftly towards the bubble's exit.

Gripping his blaster, Eileen trembling beside him, Boone followed.

Now they walked another world—a world of weird translucence, bubble-cells and tunnels, pitch-blackness and colors too brilliant for human eyes to bear.

Yet through it all, the man called Lor strode swiftly, surely. Not once did he hesitate or falter. It was as if the whole, vast, maze-like pattern were etched in acid on his brain.

Then, at long last, they were on a ramp and climbing in slow spirals, ever upward. Ahead, a pale light glowed...the light of Hyperion's ice-shell-filtered outer day.

Lor led them out a low-roofed cave-mouth...helped them up the slope of a brushy rise. Bitterly, he flung his arm out: "Look—the city!"

Boone looked, then shuddered; and suddenly Eileen was sobbing. For they gazed on a holocaust, a ruin, strewn with the smoldering shards of a thousand shattered domes.

"So these are the ways of men!" Now there was wonder in Lor's voice, and sadness. "They have so much to learn..."

"Oh, Lor—!" Eileen choked on her tears.

The mutant turned to face her. "You need not cry, my mother. We—I—shall teach them better." Then, once more smiling: "Think of some living thing—a thing of beauty. Picture it sharp and clear within your mind."

She stared up at him—face puzzled, eyes still brimming. "I—I'll try…"

"Then close your eyes."

She did as he had ordered.

Lor stood unmoving, placid. Yet while Boone watched, mists seemed to rise and gather, swirling. Then, in their midst, a flower took form, a perfect blood-red rose.

The sphere-man reached out, plucked it. "Here, my mother."

Eileen's eyes went wide with awe and sheer delight. She gasped aloud and held the opening bud close, drinking in its fragrance.

Lor faced Boone. "You asked for proof to convince doubters. Would such serve?"

Boone ran his tongue along dry lips. "Do I even need to answer?"

"Then let us go. We must reach those who can stop the blasting of these Helgae cities."

"That means the top men of the Federation. No one else could act against the Cartel."

"So, we must have a carrier." Lor smiled thinly. "Even one of Krobis', perhaps…"

Boone's blood quickened. "Yes. It might be. His base camp's near."

"Then—why are we waiting?"

Wordless again, they left the rise; and now there was new, silent tension in them—tension born of looming dangers yet to come…of the very world-shaking import of their task.

Yet other factors, even more, churned Boone to turmoil.

Could he believe the man called Lor—the incredible tale he'd told, the things he'd said?

Or, even assuming belief, could he yet trust the other? What proof did he have of the real effects of the mutation, or of the Helgae's motives? True, they had not harmed either him or Eileen. But might not that be a mere trick to lull suspicion? Perhaps Lor himself did not even know the facts. It could be that he was only a pawn—a being created as part of some dark plan to bring the whole human race down in disaster.

As for Eileen—Boone frowned and pondered. She was changed, somehow, from the girl he'd known. It was as if her basic drive, her fierce ambition, all at once had vanished. Now she was woman. Woman only.

Questions, questions. Seething, they loomed ever larger, until at last they were more than his aching brain could cope with. Of a sudden it came to him that sometime, somewhere, there must be an end to thinking, indecision.

For him, that moment had already come. From here on, if he were not to find himself forever immobilized by doubt, there could be no choice for him but action.

So, he would act.

THEY topped another rise as Boone reached his decision...looked out across a flower-field into the valley where the familiar scarlet outlines of the ramped Independent carrier rose.

It would be only simple justice were they to steal that captured craft back from Krobis.

Boldly, Boone strode forward. It was as if, suddenly, all fear had left him.

Or perhaps he knew instinctively, somehow, that here audacity might win where stealth had failed.

The flower-field fell behind them. They moved down a brushy draw into the valley. On, to the outskirts of the base camp.

And still no guards rose up to halt them. A strange, deserted air hung about the place. There was no sign of life, no human movement.

On, through the camp grounds. Across to the carrier.

Around the great ramping-fins to the yawning hatchway.

Still naught but silence. An echoing silence, too complete believe.

Eileen pressed against Boone. "Fred, I'm afraid!"

Only it was too late for fears now; too late for panic. He climbed through the port, not even answering.

Lor crowded behind him. "Let me go, my father—"

"You'll follow." Boone clipped it. "You've got a job; me—I don't matter."

On, up the ladder, then through other hatches.

Still silence. Still no sign of crewmen.

At last, the control room. Boone's heart pounding, pounding.

He stepped through the entrance.

But this cell, too, lay empty.

Slick-palmed, taut nerves quaking, Boone waved on the others.

They came in. Their breathing rasped loud in the stillness. Boone tightened his grip on the blaster.

Lor moved to the rear, to the converter chamber. "Perhaps here—" He pushed open the hatch-door.

The silence broke, then.

A thousand ways it broke: in the *whish* of a club, and the thud of a heavy blow landing; the quick scrape of feet, the blurred whir of fast movement. A curse and a clanking, a raw ring of metal.

Lor went down as a rock falls, blood spurting from a head wound.

Eileen screamed.

And then, there was Krobis: tight-lipped, sharp-featured Krobis of the too-short legs and too-slicked black hair.

Guards crowding past him, he stood in the converter-room hatchway, and never had Boone seen such malice on any human face.

"So, you traitor!" Now Krobis was laughing. "I swore that I'd get you, and by Rega, I have!"

Boone stood wordless, gripped by sick numbness.

"Chelan, take that blaster!"

A guard shuffled forward.

"No!" Boone grated. His finger went tight on the trigger. He backed to the wall plates.

"So—?" Krobis leered at him. "Think of the girl, Boone— your precious Eileen! What chance would she have, if you let go a blast-bolt?"

Eileen—! Boone turned to stare at her.

She stood slumped, face covered. Her shoulders were shaking. Wearily Boone let the guard take the blaster.

"Good!" Krobis stalked forward, still leering. "But not for you, Boone. This time you don't get off with just Venus Barracks."

Boone raised his head slowly. "Not Venus Barracks—?"

"No, damn you!" Krobis' voice rang with elation. "I'm in command here—and this is an uncharted base. Under space law, that gives me full power to try and pass sentence." A pause, electric with tension. "I'm condemning you to death."

IT was the strangest of moments. For all at once Boone's heart was no longer pounding. The tension drained from him. It was as if he had known from the start what was coming. The words in themselves brought only relief, not more panic.

Krobis wouldn't even be censured. He stood too high in the Cartel for that. Federation officials could be counted on to go along, too, if for no other reason than the trouble at the Thelema base, the wrecking of the airlocks.

Now Krobis was turning. He spoke to a sergeant: "Get a squad ready. They die in five minutes."

"They—?" Boone went rigid. "What do you mean, 'they'? I'm the one who's condemned, not Eileen and Lor!"

"Is that so?" Krobis' sharp-featured face was like granite. "You were in this together."

Fury rocked Boone. "You're afraid, Krobis; that's the answer—afraid that this whole dirty business will backfire—"

"Is that quite all?" Krobis' eyes, his voice, had never been colder. "If so"—this to the guard—"sergeant, you may proceed with the execution."

Sweat chilled Boone. "Wait..." In spite of himself, all at once he was pleading. "Kill us both, then—Eileen and me. But not Lor, there. He's a mutant—"

"A mutant—?"

"Yes. The Helgae, those structures we process—they're living, not dead. They sent him to tell us, to give us their knowledge—"

"Their knowledge? What knowledge?" Of a sudden Krobis' black eyes were gleaming and wary.

Boone sucked in a breath. "How much would the Cartel give to learn mekronal's structure—the true chemistry of it?"

"Mekronal—? This creature can make it? From basic elements found outside Saturn's system?"

"Yes."

"Then he must die..."

Boone rocked under the onslaught. He groped for words; found none.

The other kept on talking: "There are things you should know, Boone—and these guards here are men I can trust, so I'll tell you." Martin Krobis smiled thinly. "You always forget that I stand for the Cartel. We're reaching for power, those of us high in it. Mekronal is our weapon. So long as it's ours alone, that power keeps growing. Make it free to all comers, and IC's backbone is broken."

"You mean that you'd wipe out a whole culture to hold it? You'd bring war with the Helgae for the sake of the Cartel?"

"Are you stupid enough that you have to ask me?" Krobis' words dripped contempt. "We'd do even more, you fool—as witness our gambit with chandak?"

"Your gambit—?" Boone rocked again.

"So I term it." Now the other was chuckling. "Consider that report Terral showed you, for instance. I meant him to have it."

"Then—chandak—"

"—Is a fraud, pure and simple. It has no effect at all on mutation. For that matter"—once more, Krobis chuckled—"our tests show that the mutation itself brings new mental powers, not loss of old ones. But a contrary report could bring panic, help to break our opponents. So..." He shrugged.

It was a world out of nightmare, a moment to madden.

"Damn you, Krobis!" Boone choked. "Damn you!"

He flung himself forward, then, heedless of weakness, and the guards, and the weapons.

If only his hands could reach Krobis' throat, rend it—!

But a dubbed blaster hit him. He sprawled to the floorplates. Krobis' laugh rang out above him, harsh and vindictive. Death's chill fingers touched him.

Only then, in the shadows where Lor lay, his eyes caught strange movement—a slithering, a rustling, a swirling of vapors.

Numbly, he wondered...

But guards seized his arms and dragged him up roughly. Martin Krobis spat, "Kill him!" and bloodied his cheekbone.

The guards jerked him backwards, stumbling and reeling.

As they did so, the movement surged out of the shadows—and now it was more than mere vapor.

A MONSTER, it rose up—a weird, insectile monster! Great mandibles speared out, clacking and slashing.

A guard saw it, cried hoarsely and leaped back.

Too late. The thing was upon him. Claws ripped at his belly. A stinger-shaft pierced him.

Someone fired with a nerve-gun.

He died almost instantly as the monster's second victim.

Panic roared through the room, then. The guards trampled each other in their rush for the hatchway. Boone swayed off balance, deserted.

Only five in the room now: Lor, Eileen, Krobis, Boone—and the monster.

The thing swung towards Krobis.

But Krobis spun aside, not even attempting to flee; he snatched up the fallen guard's nerve-gun.

Then, pivoting, ignoring the monster, he aimed the gun straight at Lor's prone figure.

Eyes open now, the mutant jerked back—trapped, cornered.

Boone and Eileen lunged as one.

The girl was closest. Her hand hit the nerve-gun as Krobis pulled the trigger.

The charge burned out against the wall plates off to one side of Lor.

Before Krobis could fire again, Boone was upon him. They went down together, rolling and wrestling and panting. Boone could feel his strength begin to go.

But now it was not for himself that he was fighting. The fate of two races hung on the outcome.

With a curse, he writhed suddenly upward, then threw himself back, smashing Krobis' head down to the floor.

The other's muscles went slack. Sobbing, Boone kicked clear.

Then something whipped past him—the monster, all claws slashing.

Its stinger speared through Martin Krobis' brain.

There was darkness after that for Boone; a shadowy darkness that somehow was more of his mind than in the room. Dimly, he knew that the carrier all at once was hurtling upward; that the monster had vanished back into whatever realm from whence it came.

Not that it mattered at this moment. Who cared for monsters? The thing was Lor's creation, surely—a Helgae weapon he'd materialized to save them, just as for his mother's—Eileen's—pleasure he had made a rose.

Lor, their son, the mutant. Lor, first clear-eyed champion of a new and higher race.

How many battles would they fight together? What perils would they face before the war against the Cartel's greed was won?

And then, Eileen...

As if in answer to his thought, she came now; knelt beside him, cradling his weary head close to her breast.

"Eileen," he whispered, "Eileen, we have a mission..."

She answered softly, "My mission is with you, Fred, now and always."

He liked that thought, Fred Boone decided. It was one on which a man could rest at peace.

THE END

A SPACE WARP TO OTHER WORLDS

His name was Bram Forest and he had been asleep via suspended animation for a hundred years. When he opened his eyes again, he awoke as a man with almost no past—no childhood, no friends, no real memories of past events. In fact, he had no real recollections at all except one of a vague world steeped in terror from which his mother cried out for vengeance and the slaughter of his own people stood as a monument of infamy. Now thrust into a precarious future, Forest found himself in a strange world filled with terror and intrigue and under the thumb of a barbarous warrior king.

Get ready for a roller coaster ride through a rift in space into another world by two of science fiction's best authors, Paul W. Fairman and Milton Lesser.

CAST OF CHARACTERS

BRAM FOREST
Awakened from suspended animation after a 100-year sleep, his destiny was far greater than he could have ever imagined.

YLIA
Beautiful, mysterious and pure, she was the only remaining witness to a royal murder—and therefore living on borrowed time!

RETOC
A cruel and sadistic warrior king whose desire to rule the planet of Tarth knew no limits.

PRINCESS VOLNA
Her lust for power was greater than her love for her two brothers—both of whom stood between her and the throne.

PORTOX
Would his knowledge of science allow him to avenge the torture-laden murder of his queen?

JOHN PRIDE
The tale he would tell and the package he would deliver would have an enormous impact on an entire planet.

BYLANUS
He was the leader of the legendary Golden Apes. But weren't they known as just a legend?

QUEST OF THE GOLDEN APE

By
IVAR JORGENSEN & ADAM CHASE
(aka Paul W. Fairman & Milton Lesser)

Illustrated by Virgil Finlay

ARMCHAIR FICTION & MUSIC
PO Box 4369, Medford, Oregon 97504

*For more information about Armchair Books and products, visit our
website at…*

www.armchairfiction.com

Or email us at…

armchairfiction@yahoo.com

CHAPTER ONE
Mansion of Mystery

IN A SECLUDED section of a certain eastern state, which must remain nameless, one may leave the main highway and travel up a winding road around tortuous bends and under huge scowling trees, into wooded country.

Upon a certain night—the date of which must remain vague—there came a man who faced and was not turned back by a series of psychological barriers along this road which made it more impregnable than a steel wall. These barriers, which had kept out a hundred years of curiosity-seekers until that certain night, were forged by the scientific magic of a genius on a planet far beyond the sun...

The man who boldly followed his headlights up the road was of middle age with calm, honest eyes and a firm mouth indicating bargains made in his name would be kept. He pushed on, feeling the subtle force of the psychological powers against him but resisting because he vaguely understood them.

He left his car presently and raised his hand to touch the hard outline of a small book he carried in his breast pocket and with the gesture his determination hardened. He set his jaw firmly, snapped on the flashlight he had taken from the dash of his convertible and moved on up the road.

His firm, brisk steps soon brought him to its end, a great iron gate, its lock and hinges rusted tight under the patient hand of Time. It was high and spiked and too dangerous for climbing. But someone had smashed the lock with a heavy instrument and had applied force until the rusted hinges gave and the gate stood partially open. From the look of the metal, this could have been done recently—even in the past few minutes.

They were bent upon rapine and slaughter—

QUEST OF THE GOLDEN APE

and what greater prize than the Queen herself?

The man entered and found a flagstone pathway. He followed this for a time with the aid of his flashlight. Then he stopped and raised the beam.

It revealed the outline of a great stone mansion, its myriad windows like black, sightless eyes, its silent bulk telling of long solitude, its tongueless voice whispering: *Go away, stranger. Only peril and misfortune await you here.*

But I am not exactly a stranger, the man told himself, approaching the door and half hoping to find the scowling panel locked.

But it was not locked. The ponderous knob turned under his hand. The panel moved back silently. The man gripped his flashlight and stepped inside.

The knowledge that he was no longer alone came as a shock. It was brought to him by the sound of labored breathing and he flashed the light about frantically trying to locate the source of the harsh sound. Then the bright circle picked out a huddled form on the floor nearby. The man moved forward instantly and went to his knees.

He was looking into an incredibly ancient face. The skin was so deeply lined as to hang in folds around the sunken eyes. The mouth was but a toothless maw and the body so shrunken as to seem incapable of clinging to life. The voice was a harsh whisper.

"Thank God you have come. I am dying. The opening of the gate took all my remaining strength."

"You have been waiting for me?"

"I have been waiting out the years—striving to keep life in my body until the moment of destiny. I wanted to see *him*. I wanted to be there when the door to his resting place opens and he comes forth to right the terrible wrongs that have been done our people."

The strength of the ancient one was ebbing fast. The words he spoke had been an effort. The kneeling man said, "I don't understand all this."

"That matters not. It is important only that you keep the bargain made long ago with your sire, and that you are here. Someone must be with *him* at the awakening."

The newcomer again touched the book in his pocket. "I came because our word had been given—"

The dying man picked feebly at his sleeve. "Please! You must go below! The great clock has measured the years. Soon it tolls the moment. Soon a thundering on the Plains of Ofrid will herald the new age—the Fighting Age—and a new day will dawn."

While the visitor held his frail shoulders, the dying man gasped and said, "Hasten! Hurry to the vault below! Would that I could go with you, but that is not to be."

And then the visitor realized he was holding a corpse in his arms. He laid it gently down and did as he had been directed to do.

CHAPTER TWO
The Great Clock of Tarth

THE Plains of Ofrid on the planet Tarth stretched flat and monotonous as far as the eye could reach, a gently waving ocean of soft, knee-high grass where herds of wild stads grazed and bright-hued birds vied in brilliance with the flaming sun.

From the dark Abarian Forests to the Ice Fields of Nadia, the plain stretched unbroken except for the tall, gray tower in its exact center and it was toward this tower that various groups of Tarthans were now moving.

Every nation on the planet was represented in greater or lesser number. The slim, erect Nadians in their flat-bottomed air cars that could hang motionless in space or skim the surface of the planet at a thousand jeks an hour. The grim-faced Abarians, tall and finely muscled on their powerful stads, their jeweled uniforms flashing back the glory of the heavens. The Utalians, those chameleon men of Tarth, their skins now the exact color of the grasses across which they rode, thus causing their stads to appear unmounted and unguided.

All the nations of Tarth were represented, drawn toward the tower by a century-old legend, a legend which Retoc the Abarian clarified as he rode at the head of his own proud group.

He waved a hand, indicating the vast plain and spoke to Hultax, his second in command, saying, "Little would one think that this flat, empty land was once the site of a vast and powerful nation. One of the greatest upon all Tarth!" A smile of cruelty and satisfaction played upon his handsome features as he surveyed the plain.

"Aye," Hultax replied. "The realm of the Ofridians. Truly they were a great nation."

"But we Abarians were greater," Retoc snapped. "We not only defeated them but we leveled their land until not one stone stood upon another."

"All save the tower," Hultax said. "No weapon known could so much as scratch its surface."

A new voice cut in. "Quite true. Portox' scientific skill was too great for you." Both Abarians turned quickly to scowl at the newcomer, Bontarc of Nadia, who had swung close in his one-man car and was hovering by their side.

Retoc's hand moved toward the hilt of his long whip-like sword, driven there by the look of contempt in Bontarc's eyes. But Retoc hesitated. A formidable squadron of Bontarc's Nadian fighting men hovered nearby and the Abarian had no taste for a battle in which the odds were close to even.

"We defeated the Ofridians fairly," he said.

"And slaughtered them fairly? Cut down the men and women and children alike until the entire nation was obliterated?"

The systematic annihilation had taken place a century before when Bontarc had been but a child and Retoc a young man. Karnod, Retoc's father, now dead, had planned the war that defeated the Ofridian's, his winning card having been spies in the court of Evalla, Queen of Ofrid. Karnod had been fatally wounded during the last battle and had delegated to his son the task of annihilating the Ofridians and leveling their nation. This task, Retoc accepted with relish, reserving for himself the pleasure of slaying Queen Evalla. Details of the torture to which Retoc subjected the beautiful Evalla were whispered over the planet and it was said the sadistic Retoc had taken photographs of the Queen in her agony to enjoy in later years.

It had been the scientific ability of Portox of Ofrid that had engendered the Abarian hatred and jealousy in the first place. Portox used his science for the good of all on the planet Tarth, but when Karnod, Lord of Abaria, struck, no other nation came to Ofrid's aid. Then it was too late, because Abaria's military might greatened as a result of the Ofridian defeat and only an alliance of all other nations could have conquered them.

Ironically, Portox had never been captured.

Now as the tall gray tower came into view, Bontarc's mind was filled with thoughts of Portox, the Ofridian wizard. It was said that Portox had been able to travel through space to other planets that were known to exist, that he had left Tarth and found safety somewhere across space, first building his tower which would never be destroyed; that a great clock within it was measuring off one hundred years—the time on the planet Tarth of an infant's development into manhood—and that at the end of that span the clock would toll and there would come forth a man to avenge the slaughter of the Ofridians.

Bontarc turned suddenly upon the dour Retoc. "Tell me," he said, "is there any truth to the legend that the clock in the tower will toll the end of one hundred years?"

"None whatever," the sadistic Abarian snapped. "A rumor passed from the lips of one old woman to another."

Bontarc smiled. "Then why are you here? The hundred years are up today."

Retoc's hand moved toward his whip-sword. "Are you calling me a liar?"

Bontarc watched alertly as the blade came partly from its scabbard. "If we fight we may miss the tolling of the clock," he said evenly.

With an oath, Retoc pushed the sword back into its scabbard and put sharp heels to his stad's flanks. The animal screamed indignantly and rocketed ahead. Bontarc smiled and turned his car back toward his own group.

And now they were assembled and waiting, the curious of the planet Tarth. Would the clock toll as it was rumored Portox had said? Would an avenger come forth to challenge Retoc and his Abarian hordes?

There was not much time left. Swiftly the clock ticked off the remaining moments and the end of one hundred years was at hand. Silence settled over the assembled Tarthans.

Then a great sound boomed over the plains; a single ringing peal that rose majestically into the air, reverberated across the empty land that once had been the site of a thriving, prosperous nation. The first part of the legend had been fulfilled.

Then, suddenly, chaos reigned. With a great thundering that shook the ground upon which they stood, the gray tower exploded in crimson glory; a great mushrooming blossom of red fire erupted skyward hurling the assembled Tarthans to the ground where they lay in numbed stupor.

The thunderous report echoed across the plain ten thousand times louder than the tolling of the clock. But aside from the initial dulling shock, no Tarthan was injured because the crushing power rose upward.

There was an expression of mute wonder on Bontarc's face. And he thought: We have not seen the end of this. It is only the beginning. But the beginning of what? Only Portox could have known. And Portox was—where?

Bontarc started his car and moved across the plain sensing cosmic events but not knowing...

Not knowing that the sound of the tolling clock had gone with more than the speed of light across the void, had been flung arrow-straight to a brooding mansion in the heart of a thick forest upon another planet; to the door of a cavern deep in the rock beneath the mansion.

That even now the lock of this door had responded to the electronic impulse and the huge panel was swinging slowly open.

CHAPTER THREE
The Man in the Cavern

As the sound of the tolling clock died out across the Plains of Ofrid, a man opened his eyes on the planet far away and saw for the first time the place in which he had spent one hundred years.

He awoke with neither fright nor surprise but rather with a sense of wonder. He arose slowly from the great bed upon which he had lain and allowed his attention to roam about the strange place in which he found himself.

In the wall opposite the bed there was set a full length mirror and as the man turned he saw himself for the first time; a tall, broadly muscled figure of heroic proportions. Completely naked, his body was reflected as masculine perfection in every detail.

For a few moments, the man stared at the body as though it belonged to someone else. Then he spoke musingly. "You did your work well, Portox, my friend."

The sound of his own voice startled him but not so much so as the content of the words. A baffled expression touched his handsome face. Who was Portox? And what work had he done? What place was this—and for that matter, who was he himself, this naked figure which looked back at him from the glittering mirror?

The questions were annoying because he felt that he knew the answers. Yet they would not come within reach of his conscious mind.

He had little time to ponder this enigma however because at that moment he became aware of a second presence in the room. He turned. A man stood just inside the open door.

The naked one stared at the other with an interest that left no room for self-consciousness nor shame. "Who are you?" he asked.

"My name is John Pride," the man answered. He was a man of erect bearing and though there was wonder and surprise in his voice he bore himself with a quiet dignity. "And now, he added, "may I ask you the same question?"

The naked man looked down at his own body and for the first time seemed conscious of its nudity. He glanced around the room and saw a robe of royal purple lying across a chair by the bed. He stepped over and lifted the robe and put it on. As he was tying the rich purple cord around his waist he looked frankly back at John Pride and said, "I do not know. I honestly do not know."

John Pride said, "I have wondered what I would find in

this cavern—wondered through the years. Only in my wildest fancies did I tell myself that a fellow human—or even a living creature—awaited me here. But now I find this is true."

The younger man regarded his visitor with a calmness that belied any wariness between them. John Pride noted this with admiration and respect. The young man said, "Won't you be seated?" and when his guest was comfortable, regarded him with a smile. "Perhaps there are some things we should talk over."

"Perhaps there are. You say you do not know your own name?"

"That only begins to sum up my ignorance. I am not only unaware of my identity but I haven't the faintest notion of what this place is—where it is—or how I came here."

It was John Price's turn to stare. While doing so, he analyzed the younger man keenly. He saw honesty and an inner warmth that attracted him. There was something almost godlike in the clean lines of the body he had seen and in the face. These things coupled with what he already knew, intrigued him mightily and he resolved to approach this strange affair with an open mind and not play the role of the unbelieving cynic. It was time to go ahead.

John Pride said, "First, are you aware that there is another in this mansion—or was?"

"I did not even know this was a mansion. It seems only one room."

"It is an enormous structure set deep in the forest."

"This other one—?"

"A very old man. He died as I arrived here tonight."

"You do not know his name or how came he here?"

"I have a vague idea."

The young man's dazzling blue eyes narrowed in thought.

"A while ago you said you have wondered through the years as to what you would find in this room. That indicates you were aware of its existence."

"True. Perhaps at this point I had better tell you the complete story—as much of it as I know."

"I would be in your debt."

"No, I will merely be discharging the last of a very old obligation."

With that, John Pride took from his pocket a small leather covered book. He handled it gently, almost with affection, and said, "This was my father's notebook. In it, is an account of this remarkable affair, put down by my great grandfather and handed down through the line. When my father died he placed it in my hand saying it entailed an obligation both business and personal and it was my obligation as well as his.

"I have read the account of what transpired many times and with your permission I will put it into my own words. Then, when I am done, I will give you the book and the affair will be over so far as I and my family are concerned."

John Pride had settled back in his chair and was just ready to begin when the young man held up a sudden hand. "Just one moment please," he said, and a look of concentration came upon his face. Then he went on and his words took the form of a rhyme:

"An ape, a boar, a stallion,
A land beyond the stars.
A virgin's feast, a raging beast,
A prison without bars."

He flushed and added: "I don't know why I was possessed to recite that doggerel at just this moment but there is something strange about it. Strange in that I have a feeling it was taught to me at some long distant time in the past. I sense that it is very important to whatever destiny awaits me. Yet I know not who taught me the verse nor what it means."

"That verse is inscribed in this book and I believe I know how it entered your mind and memory. I believe too, that I understand how you are able to converse with me though you know nothing of this land or even this room," John Pride said quietly.

"Then please tell me!"

"I think it better that I start at the beginning rather than give you the story piecemeal. That way, your mind will be better able to assimilate and to judge."

"I await your pleasure," the young man said with impatience he strove to conceal.

"Very well," John Pride said, his eyes growing vague with a far-away look.

CHAPTER FOUR
John Pride's Story

"I AM a member," John Pride began, "of a firm called Pride, Conroy, and Wilson. We are a very old firm of private bankers with offices in Wall Street. Both Conroy and Wilson died before I was born, leaving no issue, so the company has been controlled by a Pride for many years.

"This affair in which we are interested had its inception one hundred years ago. At that time, a man came to see my great grandfather in his office. He was a most remarkable man and gained my grandfather's respect and confidence from the very first. He never stated from whence he came, being more interested in the future than in the past. He put up at a New York City hotel and my great grandfather knew there were three in his party; the man himself, another man and a woman both somewhat older than he.

"At one time when my great grandfather visited them in

their hotel suite, he saw the woman fleetingly as she was leaving the room. She was carrying something that he thought could have been an infant snuggled in a blanket. He could not be sure however and he did not ask questions.

"The man was interested in obtaining a place of abode, a place that had to possess certain definite qualifications. First, it had to be built upon solid rock and set in the most secluded location possible.

"Second, it had to be so completely free of legal involvements that when he secured title, no possible claim of another could ever be taken seriously enough to even cause the property to be visited. In short, the strange man said, details relevant to the property must integrate to a point where no one would visit it for one hundred years."

At this place in his narrative, John Pride stopped a moment to rest his voice. After a pause, the young man in the purple robe inquired, "Why do you smile?"

"At the recollection. My great grandfather had just a white elephant—"

"A white elephant?"

"Merely a descriptive term. A place that had been built before the Revolution but which even at that early time had been bypassed by the trend of progress until it was completely isolated. No one wanted it. No one would ever want it so far as my great grandfather could judge."

"Except this strange man you speak of."

"Precisely. He was delighted with the place and when my great grandfather pointed out that even with the location and the high surrounding wall there was no guarantee that wandering adventurers might not move in and take possession at some distant date, the man smiled cryptically and said he would see to it that that did not occur."

The young man was scowling. "I know that man. He is

somewhere back in my mind, but he will not come forward."

John Pride regarded his listener for a moment and then went on. "The man seemed in ample funds and paid for the property with a giant ruby the like of which my great grandfather had never before set eyes on.

"But the affair was far from ended. The man moved his *menage* into the mansion saying he would call upon my great grandfather later.

"All the legal formalities had been of course taken care of—an indisputable deed, guaranteed by the strongest trust company in the land. But that was not enough.

"After a few weeks, during which time the man had inquired of my great grandfather where certain materials could be obtained, he returned to the old gentleman's office with the most startling request of all.

"He said that he had set in motion a procedure that would terminate in exactly one hundred years from a given moment and that he wished to retain grandfather's firm as trust agents in relation to that procedure. The duties of the firm would be negligible during the hundred-year period. My great grandfather and his issue were merely to remain completely away from the property, which was certainly a simple thing to do.

"But knowledge of what had taken place must be passed down to his son and in case the latter did not survive the one hundred years, to his son's son.

"At this point my great grandfather interposed reality in the form of a question: 'I have a son but suppose he is so inconsiderate as to not duplicate with a male heir?'

"The man smiled and said he was sure that would not be the case. He was right, but whether it was a gamble on his part or whether he spoke from a knowledge beyond us, we never knew.

"But regardless—at the end of one hundred years the surviving issue was, by sacred trust, to be present in this mansion. The door of a vault beneath it would open and the trustee was to enter and deliver therein a written account of the series of events leading up to that moment.

"In payment for this service, the man insisted upon presenting my great grandfather with jewels the value of which on a yearly basis transcended all our other income combined. My great grandfather demurred but the man said nothing brightens memory so much as material gain and he did not want the agreement to be forgotten."

"What happened to the man?" the young listener asked.

John Pride shook his head sadly. "We never knew. When all the arrangements were made, he came again to the office, thanked my great sire for his services, and was never seen again."

"He must have given you his name."

John Pride frowned. "He used a name of course but there was the impression of its not being his true one. The book mentions this. The name he used was C. D. Bram."

"Portox!" the young man cried suddenly.

"What did you say?"

"Portox. The name is back in my mind. I used it as I awoke."

"A strange name."

"And stranger still is the fact that I know nothing of it— wait!" The young man's handsome features strained as he concentrated with all his power. Sweat stood out on his forehead. But then a look of disappointment came into his face and his broad shoulders sagged. "No. The knowledge is somewhere back in my mind but I cannot capture it."

John Pride was about to speak but the young man stayed him with a sudden intense look. "One thing however is very clear to me."

"And that is—?"

"The face of my mother."

"The woman who held you in her arms in the hotel suite?"

"No, I do not think so. But I see a face clearly in my mind. A sad and beautiful face. There is a marked resemblance between it and what I see in that mirror. She is the most beautiful woman who ever lived and I yearn to find her and take her in my arms."

"I hope you succeed."

A tragic light appeared in the young man's eyes. "But where is she? How can I find her? Why did she leave me in this place?"

"I do not have the answers, to those questions. But I have a theory concerning you and the elapsed years."

"Tell me!"

John Pride spoke firmly but with obvious awe. "I think you were brought here as an infant for some reason known only to the one who called himself C. D. Bram."

"Or Portox."

"Perhaps. I think you were placed in that bed and left there for one hundred years."

"But—"

"Consider. That door has never been opened. There is certainly no other exit to this cavern."

"And I have no recollection of ever having lived before," the young man said slowly.

"Yet you can converse with me. You obviously have been given an education."

"But how?"

"It is known that knowledge can be injected into the subconscious while the receiver sleeps. I'm sure the man you insist upon calling Portox was aware of this—this and perhaps other scientific miracles. Who are we to say that you were not nourished by some means beyond our knowledge?"

But that investigation was never to be made because as John Pride extended his hand to touch the box it suddenly burst into a glow and he withdrew his fingers quickly.

Before the younger man could answer a glowing point of light sprang into being and brightened and a wave of searing heat erupted from the walls of the room, searing the eyes of John Pride and leaving him to grope helplessly as in the heart of a furnace. The younger man was beyond his reach. Blinding pain caused him to reel.

CHAPTER FIVE
Question Upon Question

JOHN PRIDE opened his eyes as a moan escaped his lips. The haze cleared and he found himself lying upon a cool stone floor looking up into the concerned face of the younger man. "What happened?" John Pride asked feebly. He tried to refocus.

"I don't know except that the heat of that fire was upon us with such swiftness that we were almost incapacitated. I picked you up and started walking. Fortunately I moved in the direction of the door. Otherwise we would have been doomed."

"I am in your debt."

"No more so than I in yours."

"Did you extinguish the fire?"

"It burned out of its own accord. But only after the cave was completely gutted. There is nothing left in there but the bare rock walls."

John Pride sat up with quick concern. "The book!"

"It is gone." The young man looked ruefully down at his own naked body. "Gone—together with my precious robe."

"That can easily be replaced along with other raiment but

the book—I was supposed to deliver it—"

"—to the cavern. You did that, my friend. It was not through you that the fire consumed it. You have dispatched your obligation. Let your mind be at ease."

John Pride got to his feet. He shook his head in the negative. "No. A portion of my obligation still exists. Fortunately I did not bring forth the second and last item I was to place in the cavern."

"The second item?"

"Yes, and I believe the most important."

With that, Pride took from his pocket a small box wrapped in heavy material and sealed and resealed with a sort of rubberized wax.

"This," he said. "I know not what is in the box nor I think, did my father, my grandfather, nor my great grandfather before me. We have been given to understand that its delivery to the cavern was the most important single duty of the trust. So I now place it in your hands, praying that this act fulfills the long-standing obligation of my family."

The younger man had salvaged a portion of his robe, a length of material that went over his shoulders and draped skimpily down the sides of his body. This did nothing whatever in the way of covering his nudity but rather accentuated and added to it.

He took the box and was scanning it with great interest when the excitement and strenuous action of the preceding few minutes again took grip upon John Pride's comparatively less rugged physique.

His eyes closed and he began sinking again to the floor whereupon the younger man slipped the box hastily in the pocket that had not burned away from his robe and caught John Pride in his arms.

He lifted the elder man and carried him up from the mansion caverns and into the great hall that swept forward to the main entrance. As he walked, bearing the heavy burden as though it were but a mere feather, he was of two minds.

One mind entertained concern for his newfound friend and the other was occupied with interest in these new and strange surroundings.

Dawn had broken over the forest and in a brooding light within the great hall, he saw the withered body of the dead man on the floor. He paused for a moment and then went out across the flagstone porch and into the open air.

He marveled at the green expanse of forest that reared in majesty about him. He drew in deep gusts of the cool air and found it good. He smiled.

Then John Pride stirred in his arms and showed signs of returning consciousness. The young man laid the financier on the soft grass and watched until his eyes opened.

"Are you feeling better? Is there anything I can do?"

John Pride smiled feebly as he raised himself with the younger man's aid. "I'm afraid this has been more strenuous than I bargained for. If I'd known what would transpire I would have kept myself in better condition."

"But you feel better now?"

"Yes. If you will be so good as to help me to my car, I'll be all right."

"Certainly. Your car—?"

"A means of conveyance that will take me back to the city. It stands but a few yards down the road beyond the gate."

A short time later, the two men stood at the place that was to be the parting of their ways. Both sensed this and Pride held out his hand. The younger man grasped it firmly.

"Godspeed to you, my, friend," John Pride said. "I fear I can help you no further but if there is ever a time when my services are needed, I will be waiting for your command."

"Thank you. Whatever befalls me I will always remember you as the first friend I ever set eyes upon in this world."

With that, John Pride turned his car and drove off down the winding road. As he left, the younger man realized the older man had said nothing of the dead ancient in the great hall but realized it was because of the strain Pride had suffered. The man was still somewhat dazed from the shock of the fire.

He turned and walked slowly back toward the mansion until he stood again in the great front yard. There he stopped and stood looking up at the sun as it topped the hill east of the mansion.

"Who am I?" he asked himself. "Why was I given knowledge but not all the knowledge necessary to intelligently pursue my destiny? In my heart there is a certainty that I am an educated man. I am aware of the fact that there are different groups of people who speak different languages and I know I will be able to converse with any I meet.

"I know that there are planets and stars and moons and I know what is to be known of the universe. But where is the exact personal knowledge that would help me in my dealings with the future? Why was I left here carefully tended and provided for these hundred years only to be hurled suddenly upon my own?"

He walked slowly into the great hall and knelt beside the still figure on the floor. A feeling of compassion stirred him but there was no warmth of recognition, no personal sorrow as a result of the ancient's death.

"Have I ever seen you before?" he asked softly. "Were you—Portox?"

The dead one did not answer and the young man lifted him and took him from the hall and buried him. He could find no tools to dig the soil but located a hole that had once been a shallow well. He dropped the body therein and followed it with stones until the hole was filled. He did this with no sense of callousness but rather with an impersonal reverence he instinctively felt but could not analyze.

Returning slowly to the front yard, he pondered the dimension of time. How, he wondered, could John Pride's line have gone through three sires to John Pride, the last of the males, while he himself lay for one hundred years to emerge in his obvious prime? Or perhaps even on the near side of his prime.

He pondered this and other points until his mind grew weary from unanswered questions and turned to things of the moment.

"I know not what my destiny is but at least I am able to have a name. What shall it be?"

He remembered the one Portox had used—C. D. Bram. "Bram," he said. "That I like." But the C. D. meant nothing to him and Bram seemed somehow incomplete.

"John Pride had a name of two parts," he said, "so why should I not have the same?"

He looked about him and a breeze in the green branches above seemed to whisper the answer. He heard and considered, then smiled to himself, raised his voice.

"I christen myself Bram Forest, to be known from this moment on by that name."

Suddenly his smile deepened, then laughter welled from his great chest; a laughter arising from the sheer joy of this new thing called living into which he had stepped.

Now he stretched his arms over his head, palms upward as though supplicating to some far-off deity. He leaped high in the air testing his muscles and finding them good.

Then he was running, naked and golden off across the open hill. He ran until his huge chest pounded with delicious pain as his lungs labored for air. Finally he dropped to the ground and lay spread-eagled looking up at the sky.

He laughed long and joyously.

He lay for a long time thus, then suddenly remembered the box John Pride had given him. But the scanty garment had dropped from his shoulder's so he sprang to his feet and ran back until he discovered it.

The box was still there. He examined it curiously turning it over and over in his hands. The seal was stubborn but it finally gave and he peeled off the heavy wrapping. A small white box came to light.

This he opened to stand frowning at what it contained. An odd instrument of some sort—a flat disc about two inches in diameter and possibly a quarter of an inch thick. Both faces were of shining, crystalline metal reflecting back anything that was imaged upon them.

Two short metal straps appended from opposite sides of the queer instrument, one of which held a buckle at its end. He held the shining disc to his ear but there was no sound that he could detect.

Frustrated he looked again into the box. It appeared to be empty. But no. As he was about to fling it away, he noted that what appeared to be its inner bottom was in reality a second flat package that fitted perfectly into the receptacle. He shook it free and found it to be merely a flat rectangle wrapped tightly in white paper.

He was about to rip the paper with his thumbnail when his attention switched suddenly to the shining disc. He had envisioned a use for it; or at least a place for which it seemed constructed.

He tested his theory and found the straps fit snugly and perfectly around his wrist. He pondered which wrist to place it on and decided the right one would be appropriate.

Quickly, he snapped the buckle into its hasp and then held forth his arm to admire the brightness of the queer device.

If he had expected anything to happen, he was disappointed and he stood there wondering what use was to be found from such a seemingly useless device.

After a while he unbuckled the disc and moved it to his left wrist. Perhaps it would look better there. Again he raised his arm to admire it and had stood thus for some moments when he became conscious of an odd sickness in the pit of his stomach.

He did not associate this with the disc at all and immediately forgot the thing, giving his whole attention to the uncomfortable feeling that had come upon him.

The sickness increased in intensity and he bent down, doubling over his abdomen as the nausea became a pain. As he sank to his knees, he noted the disc had changed, had taken on an odd, transparent glow.

There had to be a connection between his illness and the abominable device and he clawed at the buckle, seeking to loosen it and hurl the thing away.

But there was no time. The pain sharpened and a black cloud dimmed his sight. He clawed feebly at the buckle and then his numbed fingers weakened, fell away from it.

The darkness increased and seemed to lift him from the ground upon which he lay. It clawed at his throat, entered his nostrils like a malignant force.

As his consciousness faded a single thought was in his mind: *Born but to live a few brief moments and die again. What sense is there to such a farce as this? Born—but to die—again. Portox! Help me! It can't be— There must be some help!*

CHAPTER SIX
On the Plains of Ofrid

JLOMEC the Nadian guided his air car across the grassy plains of Ofrid but a scant few feet above the tops of the waving grasses.

It was a fine day and the Nadian was taking full advantage of it. One of a race of proud and noble fighting men, Jlomec was an exception to the rule in that he was a dreamer rather than a fighter, a thinker rather than a doer, a poet rather than a military strategist.

Thus, his mind dwelt upon the historic incident of the previous days when, standing beside his brother, Bontarc, he had watched the gray tower of Portox the Ofridian explode into a fine cloud of dust.

And it was characteristic of the gentle Jlomec that his mind was more occupied with the romantic aspect of the incident than the violent. He thought of the poem, the bit of doggerel carved in the foundation stone of the tower. For a century all Tarthans had puzzled over the verse put there by Portox so long ago:

> An ape, a boar, a stallion,
> A land beyond the stars,
> A virgin's feast, a raging beast,
> A prison without bars.

Had it any meaning? Jlomec wondered. A thousand different interpretations had been put upon the verse over the years, but no one knew for sure.

That it had something to do with the slaughter of the

Ofridians, Jlomec was sure. But what?

As he ruminated thus, Jlomec's attention was caught by moving figures some ten jeks to the south. He knew this to be the location of one of the great wells that dotted the Plains of Ofrid.

In the times before the great massacre, these wells had been located in the hearts of the fine Ofridian cities of which the Abarians stood in great envy. These wells gushed endlessly of cool crystal water, which kept the fabulous hanging gardens of Ofrid multicolored and beautiful.

But all that was in the past. The Ofridians had been slain to a man and their cities leveled until not a stone stood upon a stone. Now lonely grasses grew where once glittered the results of Portox' great scientific genius. Now there were only round steel doors in the ground to mark the locations of the great Ofridian wells.

These thoughts occupied Jlomec's mind as he turned his car and coursed it in the direction of the well. The figures came clearly into view, causing Jlomec to frown in puzzlement.

What manner of people were these? There were a half dozen of them—two men, three females, and one babe-in-arms. Jlomec got the impression that—though they were erect and finely formed—that they were of short stature.

But now he realized he had got this impression only by their comparison to the seventh figure by the well. He knew at a glance that this seventh was an Abarian warrior, exceptionally tall and wearing the look of grim cruelty so characteristic of his race.

Jlomec paid the Abarian scant heed however, so engrossed was he in studying the strange half-dozen. Their skins were richly browned and they wore almost no clothing.

Who could they be? Jlomec wondered, and from whence had they come? Mightily intrigued, he moved forward until he came within earshot of the party. Then, for reason of the words he heard spoken, he halted his air car and frowned.

The Abarian, he recognized as the famed Retoc himself. A fierce stad pawed the ground nearby indicating how the tall, sneering commander of the Abarians had arrived at this spot. Retoc was known to roam the Plains of Ofrid at times, still savoring the destruction he and his sire, Harnod, had accomplished; pleasuring himself with memories of bodies piled high, of bloody swords and helpless cries of the dying.

Or was it for some other reason that Retoc roamed the plains? Was it a nameless fear that drove him there? Did the accusing face of Portox the Ofridian genius still hang balefully in his memory? Had Portox acquainted the Abarian devil with knowledge that he alone carried in his guilty heart? And did that knowledge generate a fear that Retoc the Abarian could not rid himself of?

At any rate, he now stood between the brown people and the Ofridian well, enjoying a useless cruelty as was his custom.

The leader of the group extended his hands in supplication and said, "We only ask water, sire. A small thing, but long have we waited to quench our thirst."

Retoc said, "What manner of people are you?"

"Harmless ones. See? We are unarmed and peaceful."

"That does not answer my question. Tell me who you are and from whence you came. Then we will see whether my fancy dictates that you shall have water from this well."

Indignation and rage dimmed Jlomec's better judgment. He had glided in beyond range of Retoc's vision and now he leaped from his car and drew his wandlike whip-sword. "Is there no drop of common decency or compassion left in you, Retoc, that you do this thing to helpless people!"

The Abarian whirled with alarm not knowing what force

might be arrayed against him. But when he saw the lone Jlomec, his composure returned and his self-assurance again took charge. Had the newcomer been Bontarc, the dreamy Jlomec's skillful brother, Retoc the Abarian would have conducted himself differently. But as it was, he sneered at the gentle Nadian and asked, "What business of this is yours, Jlomec?"

"Injustice is everyone's business. These people, whoever they are, ask only to drink." Jlomec's eyes blazed. "And drink they shall, Abarian!"

Retoc's handsome eyes glowed. No doubt as to the outcome of this contest. He drew his own sword and whipped its supple length through the air. "Since you choose to champion this scum, let's get on with it."

Had Jlomec's indignation not been of a quality to blind him to consequences, he would have perhaps hesitated. But hot with this injustice, he whipped his own sword and leaped at Retoc.

The latter, with a grim smile of confidence, parried the thrust with ease and manipulated his own whip-sword with a skill which few fighting men on the planet Tarth could have equaled.

The weapons were strange ones by Earth standards and would have probably been considered impractical. They were a good six feet in length with the supple resiliency of a fly casting rod. The trick of using them effectively lay in controlling the sway and whip of the long thin blades by skillful use of the wrist. An expert Tarthan swordsman could parry a thrust with a lightning whip of his blade, arc the singing steel in the opposite direction and perhaps bring his opponent down with a thrust that would enter between his shoulder blades, the sword still arced to describe half a circle.

In essence, this favorite weapon of the Tarthans was a

combination of whip and sword and combat was a matter of thrusting at angles far wider than could be achieved with a stiff blade. A good Tarthan swordsman would have been an excellent billiard player on Earth for his knowledge of workable angles was of necessity supreme.

Retoc the Abarian was a master at this swordplay. Enjoying himself hugely because there was little risk, he toyed with the less skillful Nadian. He did not intend to kill Jlomec, fearing the wrath of Bontarc. He meant only to teach the stupid Nadian a lesson he would not forget.

But as his blade sang and stung, its needlepoint darting in like the fangs of a snake's head, and as Jlomec's clumsy blade sought desperately to parry, Retoc's blood lust rose to the fore. The joy of dealing death to the helpless was upon him and with a swift thrust he allowed his blade to enter Jlomec's unprotected back just above the kidney, to streak upward through his body and pierce his heart.

Frightened at what he had done he jerked the blade free. Its entwined force whirled Jlomec in a complete circle from which he fell limply, dead before he hit the ground.

Retoc stood scowling at the fallen Nadian, his dripping blade rising and falling gently in the breeze as he held it extended. The Abarian's eyes darted to the group of brown--skinned folk, his anger centering upon them as he nimbly switched the blame for this foul murder from his own shoulders to theirs. If they had not been at the well—

He was ready to extend his slaughter in their direction, to wipe out the lot of them, when he paused, his scowl deepening. There was fear and awe upon their faces but they were not regarding either Retoc or his fallen adversary.

Their eyes were turned in another direction and Retoc sent his own glance after theirs. His eyes held upon what he saw. A naked man. But such a man as he had never before seen on all the planet Tarth.

CHAPTER SEVEN
The White God

BRAM FOREST returned to consciousness and realized the black nausea of his previous moments had vanished. All traces of the sickness was gone as he opened his eyes, his mind intent upon the small flat package that had dropped from the box in which he had found the strange disc-like instrument. But the package was not within reach.

This caused only a small part of his bewilderment however. His attention was riveted mainly upon the tableaux being enacted before him. A group of people, almost as naked as himself, deeply browned of skin, stood huddled nearby.

Almost as though for the entertainment of these, two grim and uniformed warriors were facing each other on the level turf before the strange circular ground-entrance beside which Bram Forest found himself.

The two warriors possessed strange supple swords, which they manipulated with much skill. At least, one of the warriors did. The other seemed clumsy in comparison but there was no hint of cowardice in his manner.

Upon closer inspection the two warriors who had seemed of a cut at first glance were quite dissimilar. The one of greater skill was dark and possessed of a cruel mouth and venomous dark eyes. The other was slim and fair with contemptuous blue eyes. He fought with an erect stiffness in his shoulders which was both awkward and dignified at the same time.

The sympathy of Bram Forest went out instinctively to the fair one but the dark, sinister swordsman held his attention.

There was something naggingly familiar about the dark one's cruel face. A tantalizing familiarity that bemused Bram Forest even as the singing swords thrust and parried with that of the dark warrior always on the offensive and the other fighter striving more for self-preservation than for aggressiveness.

Where, Bram Forest wondered had he seen the dark one before? Nowhere, of course. Any previous contact was impossible. Or was it? Dared he, Bram Forest, call anything impossible after what had already occurred?

Bram Forest glanced down and realized he had been removing the disc from his left wrist and placing it on his right. He had committed the act instinctively, in the same manner he breathed and moved and his mind went back momentarily to the two tubes he had found in his ears when he awoke in the cavern back on Earth.

Back on Earth? How did he know he was not still on that planet? I've got to stop questioning these things I possess knowledge of but know not why. I must take them at face value and without wonder. Otherwise I shall spend all my years in conflict with my own mind.

At that moment, the dark warrior's whip-sword whined in a skillful arc and entered the body of the fair one. A moan of sympathy arose from the waiting group as the defeated warrior sank to the ground, his face strained in agony and fast becoming a death-mask.

The dark warrior stepped back, a cruel sneer of satisfaction gleaming in his eyes. Bram Forest, sickened by the unequal contest rose up from where he lay and moved forward. This drew the attention of both the group and the victorious warrior and the effect was electric.

The huddled observers reacted with a mixture of consternation, awe, and fear that would have been comic under less tense circumstances. They dropped as one to their knees.

They placed their foreheads upon the ground. A concerted moan escaped them that far transcended in depth and feeling the one with which they had reacted to the death of the fair warrior.

In a language Bram Forest was completely familiar with, their voices sounded a chant of fear and awe. "The white god has come! The white god has come! The white god has come!"

Bram Forest scarcely considered them. He was advancing upon the dark warrior with the clean, stalking movements of a tiger, his great shoulders low, his magnificent legs tense for the death spring.

The dark one was frozen from surprise. From whence had this naked white creature erupted? He stood stiff from sudden fear and uncertainty a moment too long and the hands of the avenger were upon him. The fingers of those hands were like steel talons driving deep into his throat and in his panicked mind he looked upon the face of death and found it horrible. He was being driven down to the ground, lower and lower in abject submission by this strange and terrible manifestation the brown-skinned ones had called a white god.

The dark warrior's mind raced and in his terrorized desperation a native cunning sprang to his aid. Using every ounce of his remaining strength, he forced words up from his tortured throat. "Would you kill an unarmed man?"

The words touched a responsive chord in Bram Forest's mind. The craven spoke aptly. By killing him thus, was not Bram Forest doing the same thing for which he had condemned the other?

Bram Forest straightened and hurled the cringing figure from him. "Then defend yourself, swine!" he cried and seized up the dead warrior's shining whip-sword.

The dark one sought means of escape but he feared turning from this avenger as much as facing him. He could only play for time.

Rising, he retrieved his own sword and faced the other with his expression of fear not one whit abated. The man of the steel hands whipped the sword experimentally and the dark one was struck by a ray of hope. The other's actions with the blade were as clumsy as had been those of Jlomec the Nadian. Perhaps all was not lost.

The dark one gripped his blade and moved forward in the customary crouch of the Tarthan fighting man. Then elation welled up within him as the answering posture of the other revealed him as knowing nothing whatever of the whip-sword's use. The dark one's smile returned. God or not, the skill of this one with the ancient weapon of Tarth was even less than that of the pathetic Jlomec.

The dark warrior parried a clumsy thrust with ease and whipped his blade around to harass the other's exposed back. "You are a fool!" he said, "whatever else you may be. As you die, give thought to the fact that you join a large company. Those who have faced the greatest swordsman of Tarth and fallen ignobly before his blade."

With that the dark one whipped his blade home and spun his adversary expertly in order to discover the exact point of entrance of the blade. His aim was true.

It was just a trifle low but the other fell heavily and the dark warrior withdrew his blade and wiped it uneasily. His nervousness sprang from fear. If one of these so-called gods had appeared, why not two, or four, or a dozen? The Tarthan swordsman, well up on the principles of discretion, felt a sudden urge to be quit of this locality.

It has indeed a disconcerting place. Brown folk, the identity and origin of which he knew not. A white creature with steel hands appearing from nowhere. What would the next manifestation be?

The dark warrior moved swiftly toward his waiting stad. He mounted and rode away and not until the figures about the well were tiny spots almost beyond range of his vision, did he again breath easily.

CHAPTER EIGHT
The Brown Virgin

BRAM FOREST moved from unconscious into a dark half-world of pain and frustration. He felt his flame-seared body to be hanging upon the edge of a black abyss into which he could neither fall nor draw away from.

At times, it seemed, gentle hands reached out to explore but were without the strength to draw him back from the perilous precipice upon which he hung.

There was an endless time of balance in this dark half-world and then the thick blackness faded to a gray, the precipice seemed to draw away of its own volition, and the pain within him lessened.

He opened his eyes.

He was lying on a bed of soft, cool moss in a semi-dark cavern with the sound of tinkling water in the distance. He lay staring at the ceiling for a long time, wondering into what manner of place he had come and how. Then his keen ears caught the sound of breathing other than his own; a soft breathing that fell gently upon his senses and calmed rather than alerted him.

He turned his head and saw a beautiful, naked brown-skinned girl kneeling nearby but beyond his reach. He was struck first by the beauty of her face and form and then by the fact that she was not as completely brown as his first impression had given him to believe. Her breasts and loins were of pure white and droplets of shining water ran down her body.

She was in the act of replacing a sort of leather harness upon her person and Bram Forest realized she had just returned from bathing at whatever place the unseen water gurgled and laughed and that she was now dressing herself.

He held his peace until the act was completed, not wishing to embarrass her by making his consciousness known while she was nude.

After a few moments, the harness was in place and she rose to stand erect and shake out her dark shining hair. Bram Forest chose this time to speak. "I do not know who you are, but I am obviously in your debt. My gratitude."

The girl reacted like a startled fawn and drew back several paces. "You have regained consciousness?"

"It seems so. Where is this place and how came I here?"

"We brought you."

Bram Forest's brow furrowed in thought. "Oh, yes. Now I remember. There were a group of people such as you at the place I tried to fight the dark swordsman with his own weapons." Bram Forest chuckled ruefully. "It seems I did not fare so well."

"When we discovered you were not our god, the others wanted to leave you there to die but I resisted this as being inhuman and made them bring you here."

"Where are the rest?"

"They have returned."

"Returned whence?"

The girl lowered her beautiful head sadly. "That I cannot tell you."

Bram Forest smiled. "Be not so sad. The fact that you prefer to keep the information to yourself is no reason for near-tears."

"I am not sad for that reason, sire."

"Then why?"

"Because you asked the question and are even more surely therefore, not our god."

Bram Forest was deeply curious and half-amused at the trend of this conversation. "Tell me this, then. Why does my asking the question eliminate all possibility of my being your god?"

"Because if you were the god we seek and yearn for, you would not have to ask where my people went. You would know."

"Instead of clarifying the situation," Bram Forest mused, "each question sends me deeper and deeper into a mental labyrinth."

"We risked our lives in going to the place you found us. It was forbidden to credit the ancient legend of our people. Therefore—"

"What legend?"

"That upon this day and at that place our god would appear to deliver us."

Bram Forest, now desperately seeking a question that would clarify rather than further befuddle, held up his hand. "Wait. If you expected a god to appear and I arrived on schedule, how can you be so sure that I am not he?"

"We thought so when you advanced upon the hideous Abarian and took his throat in your great hands. But when you not only allowed him to live but also suffered him to take up his whip-sword and come within an eyelash of killing you, we knew you were not our god."

Bram Forest nodded with understanding. "I can see now how stupid that act was. Certainly not a manner in which a genuine god would conduct himself." He glanced at the girl and smiled. "Please come closer that I may see you better."

She moved her head in the negative, reluctantly, Bram Forest thought, and replied, "If you were our god I would gladly place myself in your power to do with me as you would, but as you are mortal, I must remain away from you."

Bram Forest frowned. "Again things get murky."

"I am a virgin," the beautiful girl explained simply and with no self-consciousness whatever. "I must remain so until my time is ordained. If I lost my virginity, even through violation that I resist, I would immediately be delivered into the Golden Ape."

Bram Forest came upright, causing the girl to retreat a step further in alarm. "The Golden Ape, did you say?"

"Yes."

"And you are a virgin—"

This last was a statement rather than a question as Bram Forest sank back, his eyes misty with thought. "An ape, a boar, a stallion—" he pondered. "A virgin's feast—"

The girl eyed him with concern. "Are you sure that your wound has not caused—"

"It is not that," he said, switching his mind back to things of the moment. "I'm just wondering—might you tell me your name without breaking any rules of reticence?"

"I am Ylia," she said with a childlike solemnity that touched Bram Forest.

"And does Ylia never smile?"

It seemed to him she made an effort to do this but was so unfamiliar with the expression that she could not manage it.

He extended a hand, not disconcerted that she did not come close and take it. He said, "Ylia, I would not again ask a question you did not wish to answer before. But I am mightily puzzled about the life you must have led—about that manner of males you have had contact with. They are certainly a miserable lot if a female of their race must look to her virtue every waking moment.

"As for me, Ylia—and please believe—I would no more touch you in desire than I would knowingly injure a child. You are safe in my presence as in the most guarded room of a nunnery."

If he expected gratitude or, a pat on the back for his nobility, he was rudely surprised. Ylia straightened, her young breasts protruding gracefully and if she did not react with anger, her face mirrored something close to it.

"Then I am not desirable?"

Bram Forest blinked. "I did not say that. You are one of the fairest I have ever set eyes upon."

This puzzled Ylia completely. "Then in the name of the Golden Ape, why—?"

Bram Forest raised his hand with a gesture of both interruption and surrender. "Please! Let us pursue this subject no further. The waters grow deep and I suspect quicksand at their bottom. There are questions in my mind. Allow me to bring them forth with the understanding that you do not have to answer any you do not wish to."

It was evident that Ylia's mind was also a bag of conundrums relative to this late candidate for godhood who had insulted her desirability and yet complimented her upon it at the same time. She moved forward and sat gracefully down near the moss resting place of her patient.

Bram Forest was aware of her tenseness. She was like a beautiful animal ready to spring away at the first sign of hostile movement on his part. But he also got the impression that coming within reach of his arms thrilled her. He believed this even while knowing that she would have fought like a tigress against any advance upon his part.

He said, "Ylia, you are indeed a strange child. You remained here after your people left and brought me back from the brink of death even with the fear that I would rise up and violate you as soon as I acquired the strength to do so. Your thought processes are difficult to understand."

Ylia lowered her eyes. "You wished to ask some questions, sire."

"My name is Bram Forest. The *sire* ill-becomes you."

"Bram—Forest," she murmured experimentally. Then she raised her eyes and there dawned upon her face the most brilliant of smiles. Her look was one of both dignity and gratitude. "You do me much honor, Bram Forest!"

"Honor? I fail to understand."

Ylia's eyes glowed proudly. "Why, you treat me with such respect that I could be even Volna herself!"

"And who is this Volna?"

Ylia was startled at this strange man's ignorance. "Why, everyone on Tarth knows of Volna, Princess of Nadia, sister of Bontarc, who is Prince of Nadia and ruler of that great nation. She is the most exquisitely beautiful woman ever to be born on Tarth."

"Fancy that," Bram Forest said with a lack of enthusiasm that proved marked disinterest. "I'm afraid I've never had the pleasure of the lady's acquaintance, nor of her illustrious brother, either."

Ylia lowered her eyes in sadness. "She was also the sister of Jlomec."

"And who, pray is Jlomec?"

"I thought you knew since you tried to avenge his death. He was the Nadian the cruel Abarian Retoc slew under your very eyes."

"I'm sorry to hear that," Bram Forest said. But the cowardly death had been accomplished and Bram Forest's mind did not dwell upon it as he could not see where it affected him one way or another.

"Ylia," he said, "take it as a supposition that I was born

this very moment and know nothing of this world or its customs. With that in mind, tell me of it—the things you would tell a wondering child."

She glanced at him strangely. "I will tell you all that I am not bound to hold secret."

"I would not wish to know more."

The beautiful Ylia leaned forward, so preoccupied with the task she had set herself that all her reserve and wariness left her. Her action brought her lowered head close to Bram Forest's face and the sweet smell of her newly washed and shining hair was in his nostrils. Then he also became preoccupied with the map Ylia was drawing on the floor of the cavern.

Long they sat thus, Ylia enjoying her task and Bram Forest's facile mind drawing in each syllable she spoke and committing it to memory.

Finally the sun lowered and the interior of the cavern darkened until they could no longer see each other. The most important conviction Bram Forest arrived at from Ylia's discourse was indeed a startling one. He was certain that this Tarth was a twin planet to Earth of which there was complete knowledge in his mind. He could hardly escape the fact that Tarth swung in an orbit exactly opposite to that of its more familiar counterpart, thus remaining invisible from it.

This conviction came to him through several things Ylia said and it was buttressed by a bit of Tarthan mythology she chanced to mention. The legend told of a flame-god, obviously the sun, which stood forth in its wrath one long-distant day and hurled two great stones at a demon who came from far away bent upon torment. This last Bram Forest thought, was perhaps a comet of great size that tore both worlds from the sun and set them upon their orbits. The existence of the mythological legend indicated too, that civilization on Tarth was not backward or at least had not been in ages gone.

In the more exact realm, Bram Forest learned that Tarth was far less watery than its invisible sister, scarcely half its surface consisting of ocean. It had two ice caps at the poles, known as the Outer Reaches and an equator termed the Inner Belt.

There were no isolated continents according to Ylia's map, all the dry surfaces being connected by wide passages of land through the continuous ocean.

Ylia's description of the people interested Bram Forest most intensely. On Tarth, he learned, there was no association of nations, each mistrusting the others in a world where a state of continuous war at some point of the globe was an accepted state of affairs which no one sought to ameliorate.

Ylia herself was hazy upon the description and number of the nations. She thought some two hundred existed but only the most important could she describe.

The Abarians were the most successfully warlike, fearing only the Nadians to the south. This because though the Nadians were not aggressive and even treated other lesser nations in a kindly fashion, they possessed an inherent fighting skill and a power potential that had not been tested in recallable history. Though they had not fought for centuries, their potential had not lessened because such a folly would have been considered tantamount to national suicide on Tarth.

There were also the Utalians that Bram Forest visualized as some sort of lizard men for the reason that they possessed the defensive characteristics of the chameleon. There was also another intriguing race, no member of which Ylia had ever seen. She referred to them as the Twin People of Coom, an area near the north Outer Reach. Bram Forest speculated upon what manner of people they would be and it came to him that the evolutionary processes on Tarth had not corresponded to those of Earth, where all members of the human race evolved into practically the same form.

Then a name came into Bram Forest's mind; a name that rose out of that mysterious well of knowledge in his subconscious; a well he could not explain but had been forced to accept. He no longer questioned it.

"Tell me of the Ofridians."

Ylia started as though he had slapped her. The deep brown of her beautiful face paled somewhat and her eyes grew very sad.

Bram Forest saw the sadness by the light of the moon that had risen and was sending wan light in through the cavern's entrance. He only sensed the paleness from the tremor of Ylia's voice. "It grows late. I must go and bring food. Your strength must be nurtured and greatened."

With that, she hurried off in the direction of the sounding water, leaving Bram Forest both bewildered and intrigued. Why had she reacted so violently to his question? And for that matter, why had he been able to ask the question in the first place? By what process did he know the name *Ofrid* and that it designated a nation on Tarth, without knowing of that nation and already possessing the knowledge for which he had begged the patient and beautiful Ylia?

Then he remembered that he had resolved not to wonder about these things—and at the same instant, remembered something else.

The small, flat package that had fallen from the box back on Earth. It had been his first thought upon regaining con-sciousness near the Ofridian well but it had been pushed from his mind by subsequent events.

How long ago had that been? He tried to assess the passage of time but failed. The only indication of its length was the fact that he bore no wound where the Abarian's blade had entered his body. That pointed to a long span of unconsciousness but perhaps there were contributing factors.

He had sensed that the mysterious Ylia had at her command something that had healed him very swiftly but he had no proof of this.

At any rate, he had to retrieve the package if possible. But would it be possible? Granted the strange disc had brought him somehow from Earth to Tarth, would it repeat the process in the opposite direction?

He resolved to find out and began unbuckling the disc from its place on his right wrist.

As he did this a sound manifested outside the cavern but he was so intent upon his task that he gave little note. Quickly, he strapped the disc into its potent position on his left wrist. Then he sat tensely awaiting the reaction.

As he waited, the sound without became so pronounced he could no longer ignore it. He raised his head and saw a tall, sinister form outlined against the moonlight. He was unable to distinguish the features, but the outline told a sickening truth. Also the drawn whip-sword spoke eloquently of who this intruder was.

The Abarian of the Ofridian well in search of prey. The cowardly assassin who would now enter and find a defenseless man and a beautiful girl whom would set him aflame with lust.

Rage threw a red curtain over Bram Forest's eyes as he struggled up to meet the intruder. But the latter never saw him because at that moment the now-familiar nausea seized Bram Forest's vitals, doubling him over.

And when the Abarian had advanced into the cavern, he found only an empty bed of moss, Bram Forest having been snatched up and whirled into darkness by the relentless hand of time put into terrifying motion.

CHAPTER NINE
In Custody

BRAM FOREST regained consciousness upon a grassy slope across which slanted the rays of a setting sun. The same sun that had warmed him upon the planet Tarth— of this he was certain.

He arose and glanced about quickly, realizing— while he was sure he had returned to Earth—that he could be many miles from the mysterious mansion under which he had spent one hundred years.

At first his heart sank because the terrain was not at all familiar. Then it rose again as he saw the tower of the gray mansion pushing somberly above the line of the forest top. He stood for a moment, orientating himself with the tower the center of his calculations. Then he moved out of the glade toward his right.

But he had gone scarcely ten feet into the wooded area when his sharpened instincts gave him quick warning and he dropped like a stone and lay still.

The sound of footsteps greatened until their echo came loud in his ears and a man passed not ten feet from his outstretched hands.

The man wore the blue uniform and smart cap of a state trooper and he was on the alert but not so much so as to detect the silent Bram Forest.

The latter, with the first moment he had had to give thought to himself since he had awakened in the cavern on the Plains of Ofrid, realized suddenly that he was no longer naked. He had of course been vaguely aware of this before but now he gave it his attention and realized what had

136

happened. He focused on past events.

During his time of unconsciousness from the treacherous Abarian's blade thrust, the beautiful Ylia had garbed him in the brilliant uniform of the slain Nadian, Jlomec. This uniform was both colorful and practical but it did nothing to either hide or encumber the great muscles of his chest, arms, and thighs.

Screaming, Ylia offered her own body in defense of her loved one.

The State Trooper passed on his way and Bram Forest wondered what he was doing about the old mansion. But this did not occupy his thoughts for long. As soon as the way was clear, he moved like a great cat through the underbrush toward the spot from whence he had made his exodus to the planet Tarth. As he skirted the last glade, he prayed that the second article in the box containing the fabulous disc he had now switched to his right wrist, still lay where he had carelessly dropped it.

He came to the edge of the open field and warily surveyed the terrain. No one was in sight. He strained his ears for the sound of any approaching footsteps and heard nothing. He sprang swiftly into the open and ran across the field.

It was there—the flat white package—exactly where he had dropped it that first morning. He swept it up, intent upon returning to the shelter of the forest.

But his interest in what lay beneath the white paper wrapping had grown to such a point of intensity that his footsteps lagged, his attention riveted upon the tantalizing thing, and he came to a full stop mid-field while his strong fingers tore at the wrappings.

The white parchment came away and Bram Forest stared at what was revealed. Then a strange and terrifying change came over him. His handsome features contorted as every drop of blood was drained from his face. His great frame shook as with an illness and such a demoniacal rage came over him as few people in this or any other world have seen.

Now a great and terrifying cry arose from his throat; a cry to make even the beasts of this forest freeze in their tracks and crouch lower in their places of concealment. A cry of such rage and agony that even the trees of the forest seemed to pause and listen in mute wonder...

Mulcahey Davis, State Trooper, picked brambles from the legs of his blue uniform and cursed his assignment in no uncertain terms.

Why in the name of law and decency had he and Mowbray been ordered to patrol this tangled, deserted spook-hole? Sure—the body of some old hobo had been found in a well with rocks thrown on it but what were he and Mowbray going to prove by tramping around through these brambles?

Mulcahey Davis heard footsteps and looked up to see Mowbray laboring across the last few yards of his beat. Mowbray broke from the last clutching strands of thorn bush and began beating burrs from his legs. "Find anything?" he asked.

"Not a blasted thing. It's downright crazy, our clambering around this woods. What will we find? A couple of rabbits?

"That body in the well has to be investigated," Mowbray said, seriously. "Pretty odd deal."

"What progress have they made?"

"They've located the outfit that held this place in trust, but the guy in charge had a stroke or something. He can't be questioned. They may never be able to question, him. An old guy named Pride. He's in pretty bad shape."

"Chances are he wouldn't know anything about it even if they could ask him. What would he have been doing out here?"

"There's that funny fire in the basement, too. Nothing routine about that. Fire so hot it melted rock. A lot of unanswered questions here."

"If they'd ask me, I'd tell them—"

Mulcahey Davis' throat froze as a terrible cry smote his ears. Mowbray paled suddenly and the two men looked at each other in instinctive fear.

But they were tried and tested law-enforcement officers and were not held in the grip of terror for long. "Did you hear that?" Mulcahey Davis said.

"Good lord, man! How could I help it!"

"Where'd it come from?"

"Over there."

"Let's go."

The two troopers plunged again into the undergrowth to

emerge at the edge of an open field. And regardless of their personal courage and experience in their line of effort, what they saw froze them anew.

A giant of a man—a creature of godlike proportions stood in the open field, washed by the rays of the setting sun. His great arms were held aloft and he was looking up into the sky with a terrifying expression that was a mixture of pain and rage.

He was speaking and his great voice echoed in what was remindful of a thunderous prayer. "I know not the purpose for which I was created but well do I now know my dedicated task. Vengeance! Vengeance such as this world or any other has never seen!"

With this the giant—clad in a strange colorful uniform of some sort—dropped to his knees and lowered his great head into his hands.

Mowbray's face was grim and alert. "Come on," he whispered. "We're behind him so we get a break. Move in quietly. And let's get him before he sees us. I've got a hunch he could lick ten of us and we don't want to use our guns."

They crossed the field softly and moved in behind the kneeling man. They acted in concert with an expertness telling of lengthy experience.

Mowbray was thankful for the way it turned out. He knew not why the giant put up no resistance. The man seemed stunned as from a great blow and before he could recover, the troopers had him bound hand and foot with their belts.

Mulcahey Davis got to his feet and wiped the sweat from his face. "There's one for the psychos and a padded cell afterwards."

"You said it," Mowbray agreed heartily. "Let's take him in."

CHAPTER TEN
The Road to Nadia

THE stads of Abaria, like the masters who rode them, were ill-accustomed to the clear cold air of Nadia. They snorted visible jets of vapor into the crisp air as their splayed feet scratched and slipped, seeking purchase on the ice-covered, up-tilted rocky plain.

"It's an accursed country, lord," Hultax told the king of the Abarians as their steeds advanced shoulder and shoulder.

Retoc sat tall and straight on the stad's broad back, his black cloak with the royal emblem billowing in the stiff wind, his hard handsome face ruddy with the cold air, his cruel eyes mere slits against the Nadian wind. "Quiet, you fool," he admonished Hultax. "Everything we Abarians say and do in Nadia must be sweetness and light—now."

The vanguard of the long column of Abarian riders had reached a rushing mountain stream, its waters too swift to freeze in the sub-zero temperature. Lifting one hand overhead, Retoc called a halt.

"They'll find out, lord," Hultax persisted. "They'll find out what you did. I know they will. They'll find out it was you who killed Jlomec, their ruler's brother."

Retoc smiled. The smile made Hultax' blood run cold, for he had seen such a smile before—when Retoc witnessed the execution of disloyal Abarian subjects. The smile hardened on Retoc's face, as if it had frozen there in the cold Nadian wind. "Dismount your steed," he said in a soft voice which only Hultax heard.

Trembling, Hultax obeyed his master's command. His stad, suddenly riderless, pawed nervously at the frost--

hardened ground on the edge of the stream. Retoc withdrew his whip-sword and fondled the jewel-encrusted haft. "If you ever say that again, here in Nadia or elsewhere, I will kill you," he warned his lieutenant.

"But the brown girl——"

"The brown girl be damned!" roared Retoc in sudden fury.

"We haven't been able to find her. That day at the cave, she came rushing out, lord, while you——"

"I was detained," Retoc said, some of the passion gone from his voice. He would never forget the sight of the iron-thewed young man, who once had almost strangled him, growing suddenly, incredibly transparent, then disappearing. He had stood there, whip-sword in hand, mouth agape, while the brown girl ran past him and——according to what Hultax had told him later——mounted his own stad and vanished across the Ofridian plain.

"But lord, don't you see?" Hultax demanded. "The brown girl knows what happened to Jlomec, prince of the royal Nadian blood. If she attends the royal funeral. She will——"

Retoc laughed. Hultax blanched. He had heard such laughter when enemies of Retoc and thus of Abaria had died in pain. "Fool, fool!" he heard Retoc say now. "Think you a bedraggled wayfaring maid of the Ofridian desert will be invited to the funeral of a prince of the Nadian royal blood?"

"Nevertheless, sire," Hultax persisted, "that day at the cave I took the liberty to send three of our best stadsmen after the girl with orders to capture her or kill her on sight."

Slowly, as a thaw spreads in spring over the broad Nadian ice fields, Retoc smiled at his second in command. Hultax too let his face relax into a grateful grin: until now he had been teetering on the brink of violent death, and he knew it.

"You may mount," Retoc said.

Hastily Hultax climbed astride his stad. Retoc lifted his

arm overhead and made a circular motion with his outstretched hand. The first of the Abarian stads advanced with some reluctance into the swift cold shallow water of the stream.

"What about the white giant?" Hultax asked unwisely when the entire party had reached the other side and Retoc was urging his stad up the slippery bank.

"Have your scouts been able to find the wayfarers who saw him?"

"No, sire. Only the girl nursed him back to health. The others fled."

"And wisely. They have learned to hold their tongues, as you should learn, Hultax. They will give us no trouble. As far as they are concerned, there is no white giant."

"But there is talk of what happened at the Tower, and of Portox' wizardry, and a god who would return, full-grown in exactly a hundred years—"

"Shut up!" Retoc cried, almost screaming the words.

But that night at the Abarian encampment a day and a half's march from Nadia City, Retoc dreamed of Queen Evalla, the lovely Ofridian ruler whose slow death by torture he had relished as the final act of his utter destruction of the once proud Ofridian nation. Evalla in the dream seemed happy and confident. Retoc awoke sweating although frigid winds howled over the Nadian ice fields. Her confidence sent unknown fear through him.

"Really, it's quite simple," the superbly muscled prisoner said in the language which was not his own but which he could speak as well as a native. "You see, it wasn't simple at all until I saw what was in the package, but it's quite simple now. In the package was a picture of my mother, the dead Queen Evalla. I am her son. I am of the royal blood. When I saw the picture, it suddenly triggered my memory-responses, as Portox had arranged. Then—"

"What about the old guy in the well?" the trooper asked unimaginatively.

"I'm sorry. I can't answer your questions now. I have to return to my home. The handful of wayfarers who alone are left of a once great nation are waiting for vengeance. I will..."

His voice trailed on, earnestly, politely. The trooper looked at the man from the state mental hospital, who shook his head slowly. They left the powerful, polite prisoner in his cell and went through the corridor to the prison office.

"Real weirdy, huh, doc?" the trooper said.

"A—uh—weirdy to you, but rather cut and dry to me, I'm afraid," Dr. Slonamn said. "Delusions of grandeur and delusions of persecution. Advanced paranoia, I'm afraid."

"It's funny, doc. When they took everything away from him he might hurt himself with, he didn't mind at all. Only the bracelet. Three strong men had to hold him when they took the bracelet."

"Bracelet?" Dr. Slonamn said.

"We got it in the office. I'll show you."

The bracelet turned out to be a small, mesh-metal strap as wide around as a big man's upper arm. Attached to the strap was a disc of silvery metal.

"You'd think it was worth a million bucks," the trooper said.

Dr. Slonamn nodded sagely. "Paranoid. It helps confirm the diagnosis. You see, out of touch with the real world, a paranoid can attach great value to utterly worthless objects. Well, I'll write out my report, sergeant."

"Captain Caruthers said to thank you, sir."

"Not at all. Part of my job."

Meanwhile, back in his cell, the prisoner, big hands gripping the bars so tight that his knuckles were white, was thinking: *I've got to make them understand. Somehow I've got to make them understand before it's too late.*

He closed his eyes, lost in intense thought. When he did so, an image swam before his mind's eye. He did not know how this could be, but ascribed it to more of the dead Portox' magic.

What he saw was the barren ice fields of Nadia, with several great caravans making their slow way across the bleak blazing whiteness toward Nadia City. As was the custom in Nadia, the prisoner—whose name was Bram Forest—knew, great funeral games would be held to honor the memory of the late beloved Prince J'lomec. And it was here in frigid Nadia, at such a time as this, when all the royal blood of all the royal households of Tarth gathered, the wizardry of Portox seemed to tell him, that vengeance would come. Here, if only…

Ylia!

The image blurred. He had seen her once. His knuckles went white as bleached bone on the bars. He concentrated every atom of his will. *Ylia, Ylia!* But now with his eyes shut he saw nothing. With his eyes opened, only the bars of his cell and the cell-block corridor beyond. *Ylia, Ylia! Hear me. There is danger on the road to Nadia. Ylia…*

CHAPTER ELEVEN
On the Ice Fields of Nadia

B'RONTH the Utalian left footprints in the snow.

Otherwise, B'ronth was invisible. But if a hidden observer watched the Utalian's slow progress across the ice fields of Nadia he would see where the ice was soft or where snow had fallen during the night into the gullies, the unexpected, mysterious appearance of footprints, a left staggered after a right, then another left, then a right again, then a left.

Actually, B'ronth the Utalian was not invisible. But like all Utalians, he was a chameleon of a man. Within seconds his skin would assume the color of its environment, utterly and completely. Thus, from above B'ronth the Utalian was the dazzling white of the Nadian ice fields; from below, looking up at the pale cloudless sky, he was cold, transparent blue.

All morning he had been trailing the girl. He had reached her camp on the road to Nadia only moments after she had quit it in company with an old man. From the tattered snow cloaks they wore, they both clearly were wayfarers. B'ronth could have challenged them at once, sprinting across the ice toward them, but he hadn't done that. B'ronth the Utalian was a coward. He accepted the fact objectively: his people were notorious cowards. The proper time would come, he told himself. There would come a time when the girl and the old man were helpless. Then he, B'ronth, would strike.

The day before an Abarian warrior had given him a description of the girl and had promised him a bag of gold for her capture, half a bag of gold if he killed her and could prove it. A bag of gold, he thought. He would take her alive. It was a long, cold road to Nadia City. True, B'ronth the

Utalian was small of stature, a puny creature like all his people. And there were certain disadvantages in his perfect camouflage. He was walking naked across the ice fields in order to remain unseen. His flesh shivered and his bones were stiff. But a Nadian boy named Lulukee, whom B'ronth had promised half the gold, was not many minutes' march behind him with warm clothing, food, and drink. After he captured the girl...

Invisible, he mounted a rise where solid sheet ice adhered to the shoulder of a rocky hill. Below him, traversing a snow-floored valley and so far away that they were mere dots against the snow, were the old man and the girl.

B'ronth the Utalian chuckled. The sound was swept up instantly and dispersed by the wind. It was a cold wind and it all but froze B'ronth to the marrow, but the Nadian sun was surprisingly warm and now seemed to beam down on him with promise of his golden reward. Shivering both from cold and delight, the invisible Utalian walked swiftly down into the snow-mantled valley.

There would be a trail of footprints for the boy Lulukee to follow...

*　　*　　*

"Cold, Hammeth?" Ylia asked her companion.

"No, girl. I'll manage if you will. Is it much further?"

"Half a day's march to Nadia City yet, I'm afraid," Ylia said. "We could rest if you wish."

The man was extremely old by Tarthian standards, probably three hundred and fifty years old. He wore a snow-cape of *purullian* fur, which the wind whipped about his bony frame and up over his completely bald head. "I'm sorry, Ylia," he said suddenly. There were tears in his eyes, which the cold and the wind did not explain.

"What for? You came to the cave. You accompanied me here to Nadia."

"When Retoc the Abarian almost killed the White God, I fled with the others."

"If you didn't flee you too might have been slain, Hammeth."

"Yet you remained behind."

"He still lived. Someone had to tend him."

Hammeth's breath came in shallow gasps. He once had been a strong, big man, but the life and the strength had fled his frame when Retoc destroyed Ofrid, a hundred years before. As a wayfarer on the Plains of Ofrid, he had aged in those hundred years. And he had shrunk and shriveled with approaching senility. "Tell me, Ylia," he asked, panting, "is this Bram Forest you speak of indeed the—the god of the legend? The God of the Tower come to right the ancient wrongs?"

A frown marred the beauty of Ylia's matchless face. "At first," she said with a faraway look in her lovely eyes, "at first I thought he was. Hadn't he come, suddenly, from nowhere, at the ordained moment? But then when he did not slay Retoc, when instead he allowed Retoc the use of his whip-sword and was almost slain by Retoc, when he bled like any mortal, when he—" All at once Ylia was blushing.

"What is it, child?" Hammeth asked.

"Nothing. It is nothing."

"Ylia. You were the infant daughter of a lady in waiting of the royal court of Ofrid. I was a captain of the Queen's Guards. When Retoc's legions brought their death and de-struction, I fled to the wilderness with you. I raised you from infancy. I—" the old man's eyes clouded over with emotion—"you have no secrets from me, child."

Ylia was still blushing. But a serene smile replaced the

frown on her face. "Very well, Father Hammeth, I will tell you. There in the cave as I nursed the stranger back to health, as he grew stronger and could move about, as we conversed and came to know each other, I—I desired him."

Hammeth said nothing. His face was stern.

"Please," said Ylia, laughing now that her secret was out. "It wasn't the kind of desire that could make me a candidate for the Golden Ape, but—I desired him. It was a pure, sweet emotion, such as I have never felt before. I wanted him. I wanted to serve him. I wanted to spend my life helping him and...Hammeth...Father Hammeth...loving him. There, I have said it."

Hammeth only muttered. They plodded on through the snow, which here was deep and powdery so they floundered sometimes to their knees.

"But a girl shouldn't feel such desire for a god, so I told myself he was mortal." Abruptly and for no reason that Hammeth could fathom, Ylia began to cry.

"What is it, child? What is it?"

"He—he fled. He had lost much blood and he was weak, yes, but he didn't even stay to protect me. He fled from Retoc. Is that a god? Is that even a man who can bring retribution to Retoc? Is it, Hammeth? Is it?"

"Yet you're taking the road to Nadia even as legend says the White God will take the road to Nadia."

"Nonsense," said Ylia, wiping away her tears. "Someone has to tell the Nadians what really happened to poor Jlomec, that's all. Retoc, Retoc will have them eating off his hand. He'll have them believing whatever he says. They'll never know that he killed a prince of their royal blood."

"But what can Bontarc of Nadia—or anyone—do against the power of Retoc's Abarians?"

"The White God could—"

"Ah, you see? Then perhaps you do believe, after all."

"The White God or whoever he was," said Ylia coldly, "fled a coward from Retoc." She pouted. "And yet, and yet he seemed so confused."

"Perhaps he fled so that the Ofridians might live again in the pride of their greatness," Hammeth declared with vehemence.

"You believe, don't you, Father Hammeth?" Ylia asked simply.

"I want to believe, child."

"You're panting so. You're tired. We'll have to stop and rest."

They were traversing the deepest part of the valley where the Nadian wind, funneling through between the hills flanking the depression, had piled the snow into drifts twice the height of a man. They hunkered down in the lee of one of the snowdrifts, where the wind could not reach them. With stiff fingers Ylia withdrew strips of jerked stadmeat from the inside pocket of her snow cloak, sharing them with Hammeth. They munched the tough cold meat, Ylia looking at the old man with tenderness and affection. Her foster father, he had been the only parent she had ever known. She closed her eyes and for a moment thought back over the years they had spent as wayfarers on the Ofridian Plain, the years dreaming of revenge and succor which would never come, the years...

"Ylia! Ylia!"

Father Hammeth was calling her name, urgently. She shook herself from her reverie. They were seated with their backs to one of the great snowdrifts, where it fell off suddenly like a suspended, frozen sea wave. With a trembling hand Hammeth was pointing before him, out across the ice fields.

There in the soft snow, which mantled the ice of Nadia to

a depth of only a few inches, were footprints. They were not old prints, deposited there when some wayfarer had passed. Incredibly, they were being made even as Hammeth and Ylia watched, as if by some creature with no palpable existence. The icy wind seemed intensified.

"It—it's coming toward us," Hammeth said, his voice a croaking whisper. Ylia knew that he was afraid again. Somehow with the advancing years, the steel and fire had gone from Hammeth's heart. Or perhaps, she thought in sympathy, the terrible defeat and destruction of Ofrid a hundred years ago had done this to him, had turned one of the Queen's proven champions into an aging craven wayfarer.

"We'll have to flee," Hammeth said breathlessly.

Behind them was the frozen wave of snow. To the right, far away across the snows, Abaria and the Plains of Ofrid. To the left, not half a day's journey, Nadia City. Ahead of them, the advancing footprints.

"Your whip-sword!" Ylia cried. "Quickly."

"I carry it, but I can't use it now," Hammeth protested. "I'm an old man, Ylia. An old man."

"Then let me have it."

"You? But you're just a girl. You couldn't—"

"Don't you see, Father Hammeth? It's only a man. A Utalian. It can't be anything else. If he comes in peace, well enough. Otherwise...here, give me that sword." But Hammeth shook his head with unexpected pride and pulled the weapon from its scabbard.

Just then the footprints became wider spaced and appeared more quickly in the snow. The invisible Utalian was running toward them. Awkward, cursing at his own impotence, Hammeth fumbled with his weapon.

You who call yourself Bram Forest, Ylia thought, *White God or whatever you are—help us, help us!* Then she hated herself for the unbidden thought. Bram Forest had deserted her once, hadn't he, after she had saved his life? What help could she expect from a man like Bram Forest? Or was Father Hammeth right? Perhaps Bram Forest had fled so that Ofrid might one day live again to see the wrath of the gods fall on Retoc and his Abarians.

Or, Ylia thought with an abrupt flash of insight, perhaps Bram Forest's flight had been out of his control. Perhaps he was as yet a pawn in a game he barely understood...

Bram Forest, we need you!

The running footprints were almost upon them.

CHAPTER TWELVE
Volna the Beautiful

BRAM FOREST had been daydreaming.

Ylia? Hadn't Ylia been calling his name? But how could that be? Ylia was almost two hundred million miles away. Clearly, as long as they kept the magic disc away from him, he could never see Ylia again. And besides, now that he had been vouchsafed a vision of his dead mother, the former queen of Ofrid, and now that that vision had conjured up the entire tragic past for him, why was it that when he shut his eyes and allowed the bright sun to beat down on the lids through the cell window he saw an image of the sun-browned maid, Ylia?

Could it be, he asked himself, wondering if somehow he were profaning the memory of the mother he had never known, that Ylia stood not for the past but for the present and the future, and that it was in the present and the unknown future that Bram Forest must live and do his life's work and perhaps perish, although he was motivated from the past?

A guard brought food on a tray. The cell door clanged

open, the tray was delivered, the cell door clanged shut. The guard did not pay particular attention to Bram Forest: he had been a docile enough prisoner.

Ylia, he thought.

He knew he must escape next time the guard brought food.

*   *   *

Dr. Slonamn held up the bracelet with the metal disc on it and stared curiously at the contraption. He was psychologist, he could hardly consider himself an expert on metallurgy. Still, he had never seen a metal like that from which the disc had been fashioned. It seemed too opaque for steel, too hard for silver. A steel and silver alloy, then? But he had never heard of a steel and silver alloy.

He held it up to the light. Like a fly's many-faceted eye it threw back manifold images of—himself. Somehow, it made him dizzy to gaze at the images. He drew his eyes away and had an impulse to fling the strange disc away across the room.

The sun was going down. He heard a clattering from the prison kitchen as the evening meal was prepared. Tomorrow, he thought, should see the completion of his work here. Another interview with the paranoid giant who had brought the disc, perhaps. The disc fascinated him.

He looked at it again. He didn't want to, and recognized the strange compulsion within himself. Then, before he quite realized it, he was staring at his multiple image again. His senses swam. There was a faraway rustling sound like—the words came unbidden to his mind from a poem by Kipling— like the wind that blows between the worlds. He gazed again at the disc. It seemed to draw him, as a magnet draws iron filings. Now he wanted to fight it, wanted to fight with every ounce of his strength. A wave of giddiness swept over him, leaving nausea in its wake. He clutched at the prison office desk for support. The rustling grew louder.

He saw—or thought he saw—a girl, a lovely, sun-bronzed girl. There was a look of fear on her face. She seemed to be crying out for help.

An abyss yawned before his feet, before his very soul. He longed despite himself to plunge into the abyss, whatever the fearful consequences might be. He lurched back, fighting the longing. Yet he knew he wouldn't win. He took a step forward…

"Give it to me!"

The voice, urgent, distant, beckoned him back to reality. It seemed a great distance off, but it was something to which he could hold.

"Give me that disc!"

He felt himself dragged roughly back, saw the abyss retreating. The rustling of the wind between the worlds became distant, a sound imagined rather than heard.

"Give it to me!"

He blinked. The nausea had washed over him. He felt weak, drained, exhausted. But the substantial reality of the prison office surrounded him.

The young giant stood before him, strapping the bracelet, which held the disc on his powerful arm. A look of intense concentration was on his face. His skin was bathed with sweat although it was cool in the room.

"What did you do to the guard?" Dr. Slonamn asked, wondering if the prisoner would slay him.

"He'll be all right. I only hit him. I'm sorry. It was necessary." The giant spoke in haste. His eyes were clouded, dreamy, as if he had taken an overdose of barbituates.

"What are you going to do?"

"You saw? In the disc?"

"Yes," said Dr. Slonamn.

"I'm going. It's my home."

The giant took a step forward, then began to stagger.

"Your home?" Dr. Slonamn gasped. "Your *home?*"

The giant, who had given his name to the prison authorities as Bram Forest, did not answer. Dr. Slonamn reached out, as if to grab him. Bram Forest stood there, a smile and the acceptance of pain fighting for mastery of his face.

Dr. Slonamn staggered back as if struck. *His hand had passed through Bram Forest's body.*

Staggering, trembling, Dr. Slonamn leaned for support on the desk. He could see through Bram Forest now. See through him entirely.

A cold fierce wind, like no wind ever felt on Earth, touched him. He shuddered.

When he looked again, Bram Forest was gone...

* * *

"Retoc the Abarian!" the seneschal's voice proclaimed.

An uneasy stir passed through the crowd of mourning courtiers in the palace chamber. Retoc, ruler of Abaria, did not often visit Nadia. A state of armed tension existed between Abaria and Nadia of the ice fields. Nadia alone of the many disunited nations of Tarth had strength in some ways comparable to that of black forested Abaria, but even then if a war came between the two nations, the issue would never seriously be in doubt.

As a matter of diplomacy, Retoc had been invited to the funeral of Prince Jlomec, although neither Bontarc, ruler of Nadia, nor his sister, Volna the Beautiful, had ever dreamed he would come.

While the crowd milled about in their white mourning

garments, Retoc told the seneschal: "I wish an audience with the Princess Volna."

The crowd was suddenly quiet. Volna the Beautiful, haughty, imperious, princess of the royal blood, would certainly refuse to see the Abarian ruler. Nevertheless, the seneschal bowed low, said, "Your request will be carried to the staff of the royal household, lord," and disappeared behind a hanging.

Some time later, in another part of the palace, Bontarc was saying: "Volna, Volna, listen to me. You can't see that man now."

"I'm going to see him," Volna the Beautiful told her brother. "So it may not be said that a princess of the royal blood hid in fear behind a wall of tragedy."

"But sister! With dear Prince Jlomec still not on the burning barge which will carry him down the River of Ice on the final journey from which—"

"Please, brother," Volna said a little coldly. "I'm going to grant Retoc his audience. Don't you understand? He thinks me weakened by Jlomec's death. Oh, I loved the Prince, yes. He was always so—so quiet and aloof from affairs of state. But I can be strong if strong I have to be."

"Then you won't change your mind?" Bontarc asked. He was a fighting man by nature. The devious paths of diplomacy he set foot on only with reluctance.

For answer Volna said: "Let me prepare to greet the royal visitor." And she watched Bontarc leave her quarters.

At once she clapped her hands. Six serving maids skipped through the hangings into her huge bower and while they clustered, jabbering about her like so many excited birds, she undid the fastening at her left shoulder and allowed her gown of mourning white to fall in a crumpled heap at her feet. She stood naked and perfectly still while the serving maids administered to her, each girl a master in one of the cosmetic arts. And Volna, she of the haughty face and glorious body, she who already had been beautiful to look upon, was soon transformed by the cosmetic arts into the loveliest woman the planet Tarth had seen since the Queen Evalla.

Her thoughts went to the dead queen of Ofrid as the maids dressed her again in the mourning garment. Evalla, a woman with beauty to match Volna's, had ruled the most powerful nation Tarth had ever known. Then, Volna smiled, why not another such woman, with hands strong enough, and vision clear enough, to grasp the chalice of power and drink deeply of its heady brew?

"Retoc," she was saying a few moments later.

She clapped her hands. The maids in waiting withdrew, giggling.

"Volna, Volna," said the big Abarian ruler. "You are glorious. Every jek of the journey from the Plains of Ofrid across the ice fields of Nadia, I burned for you." He came very close to her. His face swam before her vision, a hard, strong, handsome face with the cruel eyes of a sadist. Fitting consort for a woman who would rule the world? His lips parted...

Volna, smiling, placed her cool hand over his mouth.

"Then let me put out the fire," she said coolly, "for we have much to discuss."

"But Princess, I—"

"Hush. And what, exactly, were you doing on the Plains of Ofrid?"

Retoc's big face flushed red. Then, when he saw Volna was still smiling, he said: "When we met last, you mentioned that two men stood between you and the throne of Nadia."

"Yes?" said Volna, mocking him, turning swiftly with the light behind her sending its bright beams through the white mourning garment and outlining the seductive curves of her body.

"Jlomec is dead," Retoc said simply.

Still smiling, Volna slapped the big man's face ringingly. Retoc stepped back, startled.

"Fool!" Volna hissed. "I can call the guards. I can have you slain."

"But I—"

"I did not say I was not pleased. But don't lie to me. That isn't why you slew my brother. Well, man, is it?"

Retoc bowed his head. Only in his eyes there was fury. "We'll make a strange pair, Volna, you and I," he said passionately.

"Is it?"

Retoc shook his head slowly.

"You see? I knew it. I knew it was you when they told us Jlomec had been slain, and yet because I know you and know too how you are quick to passion, I told myself you had not done it consciously because I had suggested it to you. Fool. Can I trust such as you?"

"Only Bontarc stands between you and empire. And Bontarc is a simple man."

"As you are a passionate man."

"Yet you need me, Volna. You need the strength of my arm—and my army. What a pair we'll make!"

Volna stepped into the embrace of his big arms and allowed herself to be kissed. Retoc burned for her. He had said so. All men burned for her, she knew that. And, before she was finished, every man of Tarth would kneel at her feet and call her Queen.

Retoc drew back finally, breathing hard. Volna had for him only a cool, mocking smile.

At last he said, "There are some who might say Retoc of Abaria killed the royal prince."

"Dolt! Were you seen?"

Retoc shrugged as if it were not important. "A band of wayfarers on the Ofridian Plain. They were so frightened, they fled at once. After I had wounded the white giant."

Volna's eyes flashed suddenly. "There was someone else? You did not kill him?"

"I tried to. He escaped, Princess."

"Then you are more a fool than I thought."

"But I—"

"Begone! We can't be seen together too much. Take quarters in Nadia City, and let me know where you are. You understand?"

"Yes, Princess."

She allowed him to kiss her hand, then he withdrew. A few moments later, at her summons, the seneschal appeared. Subtly her face had changed. No longer was she the desiring and desirous princess. Instead, she was a grieving sister, whose brother's body still lay in state in the royal palace.

The seneschal, whose name was Prokliam, bowed obsequiously. He knew that by custom the body of a royal Nadian floated down the River of Ice in the company of two living servants—one man and one woman—who would perish with him in the Place of the Dead. He knew also that he had been Jlomec's favorite and now lived in constant fear that the Princess Volna would decree that he, Prokliam, must accompany his dead master on the Journey of No Return, to serve him in death as he had served him in life.

"Yes, lady?" the frightened Prokliam asked.

"Bontarc, our king, grieves mightily for the dead prince," Volna said.

"All Nadia grieves for Jlomec, lady," Prokliam said, and added hastily: "Although I must admit I do not grieve more than the next man. No, no, it is a mistake to think I was Jlomec's favorite."

"Be that as it may Bontarc grieves so that for a while at least some of the affairs of state will be in my hands."

"I hear and understand lady."

"Good. If anyone comes—anyone at all, whether wayfarers from Ofrid or others—with news of how Jlomec died, they are to be brought at once to me. Is that understood?"

"Yes, my princess." Prokliam the seneschal bowed low once more.

"Serve me well in this, Prokliam, and you will be rewarded in measure."

Prokliam smiled. "I will be the personification of discretion," he said boldly, baring his toothless old gums.

"Then perhaps I will still the rumors that you were the dead Jlomec's favorite."

Prokliam dropped at the royal feet and touched his lips to the royal toes. Then he bowed out of the room.

Volna stared for many moments at her beautiful face in the mirror. Queen, she thought. She said it aloud:

"Queen Volna."

CHAPTER THIRTEEN
The Journey of No Return

EARLIER that day, on the ice fields half a dozen jeks from Nadia City, B'ronth the Utalian had sprinted boldly across the snow toward the girl and her elderly male companion. This had taken considerable effort, because B'ronth the Utalian had not been endowed with an abundance of courage. But B'ronth was a poor man, as Utalia was a poor country; a bag of gold would be a veritable fortune to him. Like most cowards, B'ronth had one passion, which could over-ride his timidity, that passion in B'ronth's case was wealth.

The old man was fumbling clumsily for his whip-sword when B'ronth hurtled at them. The girl screamed:

"Look out, Father Hammeth! Look out!"

B'ronth smiled. They would not see the smile, of course. B'ronth, a chameleon man, was invisible. They would see his footprints in the snow, true. They would know him for a Utalian and understand his invisibility. But still the advantage of invisibility would be his. It had always been so when a Utalian fought. It would always be so.

B'ronth leaped upon the old man even as he prepared to strike out with the whip-sword. B'ronth was both naked and unarmed. The sword lashed whining at air a foot from his face. B'ronth wrenched its haft from the old man's hand. Hammeth stumbled back.

B'ronth swung the whip-sword. He was no duelist. A duelist would lunge and thrust with the whip-sword, allowing its mobile point some degree of freedom by controlling it deftly. A non-duelist like B'ronth would hack and slash, the deadly swordpoint whipping about, curling, slashing, striking.

Hammeth held up his hands to defend himself. The whip-sword whined in the cold air. The girl screamed. Hammeth's right hand flew from his arm and blood jetted from the stump. Hammeth sank to the ground and lay there in a spreading pool of crimson. His eyes remained open. He was staring with hatred at B'ronth. In a matter of minutes, B'ronth knew, he would bleed to death. B'ronth turned on the girl.

She stood before him swaying. She had almost swooned, but as B'ronth approached her, she flung herself at him, crying Hammeth's name, and they both fell down in the snow. B'ronth let the whip-sword fall from his fingers. Half a bag of gold for a dead girl, but the whole bag if she lived. She fought like a wild cat and for a few moments B'ronth regretted dropping the weapon and actually feared for his life. But soon, his courage returning and his whole being contemplating the bag of gold, he subdued the girl.

She lay back exhausted in the snow. "Please," she said. "Please bind his arm. He'll bleed to death. Please."

B'ronth said nothing. Ylia staggered to her feet, then collapsed and crawled on her knees to Hammeth. The blood jetted from the stump of his arm. He was watching her. A little smile touched the corners of his mouth but pain made his eyes wild.

B'ronth licked his lips. He had earned his bag of gold and, earning it, thought of more wealth. He thought: *why should I accept one bag of gold from a common Abarian soldier when there are millions of bags of gold in Nadia City?* He could deliver the girl, who obviously knew something the Abarians did not wish the Nadians to know, to Nadia City. He could sell her to the Nadians. Or, if the Abarians outbid them, then the Abarians…

Bruised, her cloak in tatters, Ylia reached Hammeth. His

eyes blinked. He smiled at her again, smiling this time with his whole face. Then he turned his head away and his eyes remained open and staring.

"You...killed...him," Ylia said, sobbing.

B'ronth dragged her to her feet. "Lulukee!" he called. "Lulukee!" Where was the boy?

Lulukee did not answer. Cursing, B'ronth stripped the corpse and dressed in its warm clothing. The blood on the right sleeve was already stiff with cold. Where could Lulukee have gone off to? wondered B'ronth. Well, no matter. They were only a few jeks from Nadia City, where wealth awaited him...

"Come," he said. He dragged the girl along. She looked back at the dead old man until a snowdrift hid him from sight.

After the Utalian had dragged the beautiful girl beyond the ridges of snow, Lulukee the Nadian came down into the valley. He was a small boy of some sixty winters who, like many of the Nadians who did not come from their country's single large city, had lived a hard life as an ice field nomad. He had seen an opportunity to profit in the service of B'ronth the Utalian, but had not expected this service to include murder. Thus when the Utalian had called him, expecting the boy to drag his supply sled down into the snow-valley, Lulukee had remained hidden. Now; though, he made his way to the body of the dead man and, scavengerlike, went over it with the hope of turning a profit by B'ronth's deed.

In that he was disappointed. B'ronth had taken the dead man's snow cloak and his whip-sword: there was nothing left for Lulukee's gleaning. He was about to turn and trudge back the way he had come, when he realized that if he did so, if he exposed himself on the higher wind-ridges, B'ronth might see him. Therefore he remained a long time with the frozen body of Father Hammeth, actually falling into a light slumber while he waited.

He awoke with a start. He blinked, then cowered away from the apparition, which confronted him. It was a man, but such a man as Lulukee the Nadian had never seen before, a superbly muscled man a head taller than the tall Abarians themselves.

"Where's the girl?" the man demanded.

"I—I don't know, lord."

"How did this happen?" The man looked down with compassion at Father Hammeth's corpse.

"I only just arrived, l-lord."

"You lie," the big man said. "You were sleeping here. You'll tell me, or—"

Lulukee blanched. He owed no loyalty to B'ronth the Utalian. If indeed he remained loyal he might be implicated in the murder of the old man. He said: "It was B'ronth the Utalian."

"Where is he?"

"G-going to Nadia City, I think."

"Alone?"

"No, lord. With his prisoner. A—a lovely woman."

"Ylia!" the giant cried. "You! How are you called?"

"I am Lulukee of Nadia, lord."

"Lead me to the city. Lead me after them."

"But lord—"

"Lead me." The giant did not shout. He did not menace of glower or threaten. Yet there was something in his bearing which made it impossible for the frightened Lulukee to do anything but obey. "Yes, lord," he said.

"Tell me—" as they started out, the boy's sled reluctantly left behind—"is this B'ronth the Utalian in Retoc's pay?"

"No, I don't think so. He works alone, lord. Reaping

profit wherever he can."

"And he took the girl unwillingly?"

"Yes, lord."

"He won't profit in this venture," Bram vowed.

The wind howled behind them. Six jeks ahead of them was Nadia City.

*　　*　　*

"Can't you see I'm busy? Can't you see I have no time for the likes of you?" Prokliam the seneschal whined in self-pity.

"Then make time," B'ronth said boldly, his cowardice obscured by dreams of avarice. "What I have brought through the Ice Gates is important to your ruler."

"Bontarc of Nadia," said the seneschal haughtily, "does not waste his time on every Utalian vagabond who reaches his court."

"True. But I assume Bontarc of Nadia wishes to know exactly how his brother, the Prince Jlomec, died?"

Prokliam fought to keep his puckered old face impassive. But his mind was racing and his heart throbbed painfully. Could the Utalian know anything about that? If so, and if he, Prokliam, brought this B'ronth before the Princess Volna as she had ordered...

"Wait here," Prokliam snapped arrogantly. "And keep your cloak on. We don't want invisible Utalians floating about the palace."

B'ronth offered a mock bow. Prokliam turned to go, then whirled about again. "If you're lying, wasting my time—"

B'ronth smiled unctuously. "In the ante-room, being amused by your palace guards, is one who has been on the Plains of Ofrid quite recently."

"So?"

"When the Prince Jlomec was there. She saw him slain."

165

"Wait here," said Prokliam a little breathlessly. He pushed the hanging aside and stalked down a corridor, and around a bend, and up a flight of stone stairs. He was busy, all right. That had been no lie. Preparations must be made for the funeral games of the Prince Jlomec, to which all the nobility of Tarth had been invited. But this, obviously, was more important. On this Prokliam's life might depend...

"Are they checking waypasses, lord?" Lulukee asked the big, silent man at his side. Ahead of them, filing slowly through the Ice Gates, were hundreds of visitors entering Nadia City for the funeral games. A flat-bottomed air car hovered overhead, peltasts leaning over its sides, ready. Guards flanked the Ice Gates with drawn whip-swords, as if admitting the superiority of Abarian weapons of war.

"We'll get through," Bram Forest vowed. "Tell me, Lulukee, if you brought a prisoner to the city who might be worth much to the Abarians but also to the Nadians, and if you were intent on getting the biggest profit, where would you take her?"

"If I had great courage, lord?"

"If you dreamed of reward."

"I would take her to the royal palace, lord, to Bontarc the King or to his sister, Princess Volna the Beautiful, who, some say, is the real power behind the Nadian throne although Bontarc is a great soldier."

They had reached the gate. "Way passes," a bored guard said.

Lulukee mumbled something uncertainly. His heart beat painfully against his ribs. His brain refused to function. There was intrigue here, he could sense that. More intrigue than he cared to have a hand in. As a Nadian citizen, he owned a way pass, of course. But the giant? Obviously the giant did not. Lulukee was sorry he had ever agreed to go along with B'ronth the Utalian. Now he only wanted to get out of the entire situation as quickly—and safely—as possible.

He pointed an accusing finger at Bram Forest. "*He* has no way pass!" Lulukee cried.

The guards stiffened, their whip-swords ready. They looked at Bram Forest. Overhead, the air car hovered, its peltasts stationed there in the event of trouble, their slings poised.

Ylia was in there somewhere, a prisoner. Bram Forest spurned violence for its own sake, but Ylia might need him. Ylia, who had nursed him back to health when Retoc had left him for dead on the parched Plains of Ofrid. Ylia, the lovely.

"I'm going through," Bram Forest said softly. "Don't try to stop me."

For answer, the nearest guard let his left hand drop.

It had been a signal. Overhead, the peltasts drew back their slings. "Will you go in peace?" the guard asked, his eyes narrow slits now, his right arm tensed to bring the whip-sword around.

Bram Forest waited. Every muscle in his superbly conditioned body cried for action, but he would not initiate it.

The guard pointed back along the path across the ice fields, where hundreds of visitors to the city were waiting impatiently. "Then go," he said harshly, "before your flesh feeds the stiltbirds on the banks of the River of Ice."

The guard raised his sword menacingly. Standing rigidly still and giving no warning, Bram Forest lashed out with his left fist, hitting the guard in the mouth. Lips split, teeth flew, blood covered the guard's face. Someone screamed. The guard fell, but his companion lashed out with his own whip-sword. Bram Forest lunged to one side and grabbed the sword-arm, twisting it. The guard howled, dropping his weapon. Lulukee made a dive for it. But the guard, his legs still free, kicked Lulukee in the face. As he fell, his senses blurring, Lulukee wondered why he had made that desperate, foolish attempt to help the big, silent man. He could not answer the question in mere words. But there was something about him, something about Bram Forest, which drew loyalty from you even as the sun drew dew from the ground...

Bram Forest lifted the second guard by sword-girdle and scruff of neck and held him aloft. The guard's arms and legs flailed frantically. "No!" he screamed up at the peltasts. "No..."

But they had already unleashed their first volley of stones, pelting the helpless guard until he lost consciousness. Bram Forest flung him aside, leaped over the first fallen guard's supine body, and plunged recklessly into the crowds milling just inside the Ice Gates.

"He went that way!" a voice screamed.

"That way!"

"Over there!"

"There he is!"

It was an ancient city, with narrow, tortuous alleyways and overhanging buildings and little-used passageways. The wide streets—the few there were—mobbed with people.

For all his size, the giant had disappeared.

Lulukee picked himself up, dusted himself off, and showed his way pass to the guard. The guard said nothing. He had lost three teeth and his mouth was swollen, painful. Lulukee sensed that somehow the little he had done to help Bram Forest was all he would ever do for him. Yet he felt with a strange pride he did not fathom that although his role in the saga of the mysterious giant had come to an end, it was the most important event in his life and would remain so if he lived to be six-hundred. He felt somehow—and could not explain why he felt this—as if in his small way he had done something to make the world Tarth a better place in which to live.

Whistling, he pushed his way through the crowds and was lost to sight just as the giant who went before him.

*   *   *

"B'ronth of Utalia!" Prokliam the seneschal proclaimed. Volna the Beautiful nodded. The doddering old seneschal had already told her about the Utalian. She was prepared to receive him now. If he knew what he claimed to know, if he knew the true details of the death of Prince Jlomec, then he must be silenced. Naturally, he wanted gold. They always wanted gold. But gold was not the way to silence them. Gold never worked. It only made them greedy for more.

With Volna were, instead of her usual ladies in waiting, two discreet palace guards. Grinning, she looked at their whip-swords. That was the way to silence one such as B'ronth the Utalian.

"He may enter," Volna told the seneschal. Prokliam bowed out, saying:

"And Princess, you will not forget—"

"No, Prokliam, I won't forget. You hardly knew the Prince Jlomec at all, did you? You certainly couldn't have been his favorite."

"Princess," breathed the seneschal tremulously as he withdrew.

A moment later, B'ronth the Utalian entered the royal chamber. He wore a snowcloak. He was all but invisible except for the snow-cloak. He was, eerily, a disembodied cloak floating through air. Although, noticed Volna, if you looked closely you could see the faintest suggestion of a man's head above the cloak, as if you saw the rich wall tapestries of the room through a transparent, headshaped glass. Likewise, the suggestion of arms and legs...

"You are B'ronth?" An unnecessary question, but Volna had not yet made up her mind what must be done.

"Yes, majesty," the cloak said in a different but somehow unctuous voice.

"You are alone?"

"No, majesty," said the cloak.

"Then—?"

"A girl. A wayfarer of the Plains of Ofrid. I accompany her."

"And the story you have to tell?"

"I realize, majesty, how the royal Princess must grieve at the loss of her royal brother, the Prince. I realize..."

"To the point, man. Get to the point. Are you trying to say you know how Prince Jlomec was slain? You know who killed him?"

"Yes," said the cloak boldly, eagerly.

Princess Volna smiled. Perhaps something in that smile warned B'ronth the Utalian. But of course, the warning came too late. In a quick jerky motion, the cloak retreated toward the doorway. "Princess..." B'ronth said.

Princess Volna told her guards: "Kill him."

B'ronth the Utalian had time for one brief scream which, if a sound could, seemed to embody all his frustrated dreams of wealth. Then one of the guards moved swiftly, his arm streaking out. The whip-sword in his hand lashed, blurring, toward the cloak. Bright red blood welled, jetted.

B'ronth the Utalian's head, no longer invisible, rolled on the floor at Volna's lovely feet. "Clean that up," she told one of the guards. To the other she said: "Now fetch the girl."

"Mind, lord, I don't question you," Hultax the Abarian said. "But it's just—"

"Did you send the message?" Retoc cut him off.

"As you ordered, sire. Yes."

"Good."

"Sire, I hate inactivity. I loathe it. I am a soldier."

"As I am," said Retoc slowly, his hard cruel eyes staring at something Hultax couldn't—and would never be able to—see.

"So we just sit here in this rented house in Nadia City, cooling our heels. It doesn't make sense, sire."

"Sense?" mused Retoc. "What is sense? Is it victory and power for the strongest? Well, is it?"

"Yes, lord," Hultax responded." But—"

"And you sent the message? Our legions will come?"

"Yes, lord. Two days hence they'll be encamped on the ice fields three jeks march from the city gates. But I don't see—"

"You obey, Hultax. I see. I do the seeing."

"But I thought you...the Princess Volna...together..."

"The Princess can serve me, now. If she can deliver Nadia without a fight then Tarth is mine, Hultax, don't you see? In two days all the royal blood of all the royal families of Tarth will be assembled here in Nadia for the funeral games. If Bontarc's army doesn't interfere, then I will be master of Tarth."

"But if Bontarc finds out—"

"That, Hultax," said Retoc with a smile, "is why you sent the message."

"My sire," said the proud soldier Hultax humbly.

Soon, thought Retoc, all Tarth would call him that. *My sire...*

*   *   *

Ahead of Bram Forest loomed the ramparts of the palace. He must hurry. He knew he had to hurry. He pushed impatiently through the crowd. Several times men looked up angrily, and would have said something. But when they saw his face, they turned away.

What they saw in Bram Forest's face made them afraid.

"Majesty!" Prokliam the seneschal said.

"Well?" Volna demanded. "Didn't the guards send you for the girl?"

"Majesty, I was thinking…"

"Well, Prokliam, what is it? Didn't you go for the girl?"

"Not yet, majesty, begging your pardon…"

"If you have something to say, then say it. And get the girl."

"Majesty, a seneschal knows the palace. It is his job…"

"I warn you, Prokliam, I have little patience today." Her anxiety was evident.

"No one wishes to be chosen," Prokliam blurted quickly, boldly, "even as I did not wish to be chosen to accompany the body of Prince Jlomec on the Journey of No Return. Now that you have spared me, in your royal benevolence, I thought I might in turn advise you…"

"Yes, what is it, man?"

"You should not have killed the Utalian, majesty. If it is ordained that a living man and a living woman accompany the Prince's body to the Place of the Dead, to die there with him, their spirits serving him in death, why choose from among the palace staff? We all have family, we all have friends, we all stand something to lose. But majesty, if you were to break with tradition, if you were to send instead two strangers whose loss meant nothing to the palace, the palace staff would love and revere you even more than they already do."

Volna's beautiful face smiled at him. He did not know what she was thinking. He never knew. No one did. She might reward him or have him slain on the spot. "Why do you tell me this, Prokliam?" she asked.

"For saving me when it was thought I would accompany—"

"No. There must be another reason."

"If you do this deed and if the palace and the people love you for it, and if the scepter of power should slip from Bontarc's hand to yours, and if, when it came time to select your prime minister…"

"Ha! Ha! Ha! We have an ambitious palace butler."

"But surely you—"

"Yes, Prokliam. I understand. I won't deny it. Perhaps I had the Utalian slain impetuously. But there's still the girl."

"I'll fetch her at once, majesty."

"And if," mused Volna, no longer aware of the seneschal's presence, "we could find another stranger, a man, to accompany the body of Prince Jlomec on the Journey of No Return, not only the palace, but the people as well would love me. A stranger…"

"Take me to your King," Bram Forest told the palace guard.

The guard smirked. "Do you think any stranger in the realm is granted an audience with King Bontarc, fool?"

"It is a matter of life and death."

"But whose life and death?" demanded the guard, roaring with laughter. "Yours, idiot?"

"It is about Ylia the Wayfarer."

"I know of no Ylia the Wayfarer. Begone, dolt!"

"It is about Prince Jlomec." The guard's eyes narrowed.

The word had been passed by no less a person than Prokliam the seneschal that anyone with information concerning the death of the royal Prince should be brought at once not to Bontarc but to Princess Volna. Could the guard, could he, Porfis, do less?

"Very well," he said. "Come with me."

Unarmed, but aware of his giant's strength and the mission which had seen him spend the first hundred years of his life in a crypt on Earth, Bram Forest went with the guard.

The way was long, through chambers in which priceless tapestries hung, through narrow, musty corridors into which the light of day barely penetrated, through rooms in which ladies in waiting and courtiers talked and joked, up bare stone stairs and through heavy wooden doors which Porfis the guard opened with a key which hung at his belt. The doors opened slowly.

Bram Forest entered a large room. It was, he could see at a glance, a woman's bower. Someone was standing at the far end of the room, in shadow. He squinted. He took two slow steps into the room. He began to run.

"Ylia! Ylia!" he cried.

Too late he saw the fetters binding her arms. Too late he saw her bite savagely at something and twist her neck and spit the gag from her mouth. Too late he heard her cry:

"Bram! Bram Forest! Behind you!"

He turned barely in time to see Porfis the guard, his whip-sword raised overhead hilt-first. He lifted his arm, but it was swept aside in the downward rush of the sword. Something exploded behind his eyes and all eternity seemed to open beneath his feet. He plunged into blackness with Ylia's name on his lips.

Unconscious, he was taken with Ylia through subterranean passages to the Royal Dock on the River of Ice. The barge with Jlomec's embalmed body waited. It was very cold on the river. The Place of the Dead beckoned from the unseen end of the Journey of No Return.

CHAPTER FOURTEEN
Land Beyond the Stars

AT FIRST Retoc the Abarian was too stunned by what he witnessed to think coherently. With the other Tarthians of royal blood he had received an unexpected summons to appear at the Royal Dock on the River of Ice and, before he could even try to fathom what it was about, an escort of Nadian guards had come to fetch him.

It was cold and murky on the banks of the River of Ice. The two men, Retoc and Hultax had arrived barely in time to see them unfastening the hawsers of the Royal Barge. Curious, he pushed closer through the crowd of nobles. Suddenly, before the barge was quite unmoored, as it swayed and rocked on the currents of the river, Nadian soldiers appeared with a platform on poles slung across their shoulders, the usual means of intra-city transportation for Nadian royalty. But this was no royalty Retoc saw on the platform, although they were dressed as royalty.

The woman, conscious and bound hand and foot, was the Virgin of the Wayfarers who had witnessed Prince Jlomec's death. The man, unconscious, his head propped high on pillows, was the white giant who once on the Plains of Ofrid had almost strangled Retoc.

A hatred such as he had never known flashed through Retoc's brain. He was so close he could see the gentle up--and-down motion of the giant's chest as he breathed. Then, beyond the platform, he saw Volna. Volna smiled at him. The platform bobbed by, was placed on the barge at the foot of Jlomec's bier. The remaining hawsers were cut loose.

There was, Retoc thought triumphantly, no return from

the Place of the Dead.

But still, the white giant had recovered from what looked like certain death once, had vanished abruptly and fantastically when he would have died again. What was good enough for Volna the Beautiful was not necessarily good enough for Retoc of Abaria. He watched only long enough to see the royal barge pushed out into the icy currents of the river, then he turned and made his way to the second tier of observers, where Hultax stood among the lesser nobility and the military officers of the planet Tarth. He found Hultax and whispered for a time in his ear.

Hultax's face blanched. "But lord," he protested, "there is no return...it is obvious the man will die...you couldn't expect me to..." Hultax, frightened, confused, could neither think clearly nor express himself properly. His mouth hung open.

"Earlier, Hultax," Retoc said with a hard smile, "you craved action. I give you action. Take a boat. There are some moored down-river for the use of Nadian priests on their religious pilgrimages to the banks where the stiltbirds dwell. Overtake the royal barge. Board it. Slay the man and the woman."

"But I—the Place of the Dead..."

"Fool!" hissed Retoc. "I didn't ask you to visit the Place of the Dead. That's up to you. If you slay them first, on the River of Ice, and can bring back proof...but the longer we talk, the further they are. You'll go?"

It was phrased as a question; actually, it was a command. Grim-faced, the whip-sword trailing at his side, Hultax left the crowd of soldiers and made his way downstream. A few moments later he had poled a wooden skiff out into the icy current and went down-river in pursuit of the royal barge.

The guards had unbound Ylia's fetters on the barge, knowing she could never swim for safety in the waters of the

River of Ice. She sat now at the foot of Jlomec's bier, with Bram Forest's handsome head cushioned on her lap. It was very cold there on the river. Wind blew, rustling the reeds, which grew along the bank. They had long since emerged from the river's underground cavern. The swift current carried them now through a country of ice, a tundra. The reeds, twice as tall as a man, seemed to thrive on the riverbanks. They swallowed everything.

Bram Forest opened his eyes, and looked at her, and smiled. He tried to sit up, wincing as pain knifed through his head. "We seem to make a habit of this," he said, smiling again.

"Shh, you mustn't talk."

She leaned close. He could smell the animal perfume of her body, like musk and jasmine. Impulsively, she kissed him softly on the lips. His arm went around her neck. He pulled her head down and drank deeply of her.

"Why..." she began, all breathless.

"Because I love you. I think I loved you the first moment I saw you. But I didn't know it then." He laughed softly, gently, and she did not know why this should be so.

"Why do you laugh?"

"I was an infant, the son of the Queen. Of Queen Evalla. Portox the scientist fled with me, the last of the royal Ofridian blood, to the other side of the solar system, to a world the twin of this, a world we never see because the sun always stands between us, a world called Earth. There I would wait until maturity. There I would be given the strength and the wisdom I needed. And then I would return to Tarth and right the ancient wrong. Well, I have returned. I love you. It is enough, Ylia. I want to think of the future, not the past."

Ylia let him kiss her again. "Isn't it the same, the future and the past? Aren't they one? I too am of Ofridian blood,

Bram Forest, of the lesser nobility. There are hundreds of us, living nomadic lives on the Ofridian Plains, where once our great nation stood."

"I didn't know that. It wasn't in Portox's training. Now Portox is dead. I buried him on this world called Earth. He could not even come back to his native Tarth."

"Darling, don't you see? That's exactly why the ancient wrong must be righted, why Retoc must pay for his infamous deeds. So Portox and the millions of other Ofridians, slain, all slain, can sleep eternally in peace. You are their champion."

"But revenge? What is revenge if—"

"You are the champion of the future too! Don't you see, oh, don't you? Of all the unborn tomorrows when the Ofridian nation may live again. Of all the unborn tomorrows when the nations of Tarth can live together in peace and harmony. Don't you understand that?"

"It's funny. I try to see my mother's face. Queen Evalla. But all I see is you. She's the past, Ylia. You're the future." He held her lightly.

"There is no future for anyone as long as Retoc the Abarian rules, and dreams of Tarth, all Tarth, as his domain."

Bram Forest stood up. The cold winds blew. He looked at the blue-cold body of Jlomec, lying in state, at the ice-choked river, at the banks of rustling reeds. He did not have to ask where they were. He knew. "Perhaps," he said at last. "I only mean that if I do this thing it will be more to see that future generations live in peace than to bring vengeance on a power-mad Abarian."

"Oh, Bram! That's what I wanted you to say. I wanted to hear you say that. For tomorrow! For all our tomorrows."

Bram Forest walked to the rail of the barge, and gripped it, and looked out over the ice-flows. He recited:

"An ape, a boar, a stallion,
A land beyond the stars.
A Virgin's feast, a raging beast,
A prison without bars."

"Why, what an unusual poem!" Ylia cried. Then: "Hold me close, it's so cold. And I'm afraid, Bram Forest…"

"Of the Place of the Dead?"

"Yes, yes. The Place of the Dead."

"It and the poem are entwined," Bram Forest said musingly. "I know they are. Together, they're my destiny."

"And the destiny of all Tarth?"

"Perhaps. Portox liked to think so, I guess."

"I like to think so, Bram Forest." She smiled up at him tremulously. "And my destiny as well."

"Ylia," he asked abruptly, "what do you know about the Golden Ape? You mentioned it to me once, when you thought I…well, when you thought I endangered your virginity."

"Why, nothing beyond what the legends say."

"And what do the legends say?"

"It is written in the most ancient of our religious beliefs that the messenger to the Place of the Dead is a Golden Ape. Naturally, in these same beliefs, a defiled virgin is supposed to kill herself. Thus, in a way of speaking, she goes to the Golden Ape. You see?"

Bram Forest smiled down at her. "What would you think if I told you the Golden Ape was real? If I told you that there actually was a Place of the Dead?"

"For the spirits of the departed?" Ylia asked in a very small voice.

"No. Man can't presume to know about that. It's in the realm of the gods. I mean a place, which somehow borders on Tarth and yet…yet is beyond the stars. A place which, when wayfarers returned from it miraculously long and long ago, gave rise to the legends."

"Borders on Tarth…yet beyond the stars? How can this be?"

"Portox found it and explained it with his science," Bram Forest insisted. "Earth and Tarth, twin worlds, yet so different, forever unseen one by the other, on opposite sides of the sun. They're unique in the solar system, Ylia. Portox thought—if the memory he planted in my mind is correct— that they're unique in the entire universe. Somehow, a million million years ago, a world split, becoming two worlds. But ordinary space…I don't know, the memory is confused…could not hold them. There is a warp of space, a place where space bends. Learn to master the warp and you go instantly from Tarth to Earth, or back again. That was the way Portox brought me, as an infant, to Earth." He held aloft his arm, showing her the steel-silver disc. "With this I can travel back and forth at will. Without it, either Earth or Tarth would be my prison…" His voice trailed off.

Then he blurted: " 'A prison without bars!' "

"What…"

"The prophetic poem. Part of the poem. Anyway, Ylia, Earth and Tarth exist at either end of this space warp, connected thus through normal space where there should be no connection. And someplace along the warp—where ordinary space-time distances don't matter…"

"I'm sorry, Bram Forest. I don't understand you."

"I'm not sure I understand myself. Tarth is a primitive world. It is beyond our science. It is even beyond the science of Earth, I believe, and Earth is a millennium ahead of Tarth in its development. But Portox knew. Anyhow, someplace along the warp—in ordinary distances along the space-time continuum perhaps a billion light years distant from either Earth or Tarth, is a third world. On the warp it is very close. The River of Ice leads to it. We call it the Place of the Dead."

"But the Golden Ape—?"

"—inhabits the so-called Place of the Dead. Their world was dying, but Portox saved them. I think...the science is beyond me...the entropy of their galaxy was running down...their world perishing, freezing...when somehow with his great science Portox claimed for their use the unavailable energy in their...their themodynamic system, and saved them."

"Why do you frown so?"

"Words. Words only. I don't understand. I can only act."

"You can act," Ylia said, hugging herself tight against him. "For Tarth and the future."

"For Tarth and the future," Bram Forest said, but he hardly heard the words.

Ahead of them in the cold clear air a wall seemed to rise. It came up so suddenly, and, in fact, the air had cleared so suddenly from the accustomed murkiness, that Ylia was afraid. "It is in the legend," she whispered. "The Black Wall, Bram Forest. And beyond it—the Place of the Dead."

"More accurately, an edge-on view of the space-warp, where it meets the normal world." But although he spoke the words of Portox, Bram Forest did not sound too confident.

"We're coming closer to it, Bram. Hold me!"

He held her. There was nothing else he could do. The current swept the barge on inexorably. The Black Wall reared ahead of them, frowned down at them, seemed to block off all the rest of the universe and all reality whether of Earth or of Tarth...

The barge penetrated the wall. Black and solid-seeming,

solid as stone, it yet offered no resistance. The barge disappeared within it.

Behind the barge, rope-trailing so close that its prow almost scraped the royal wood, was a skiff in which, shaking and afraid yet somehow triumphant because he had heard Bram Forest's strange words, was Hultax the Abarian.

CHAPTER FIFTEEN
The Golden Ape

HULTAX the Abarian shook himself. He had lost consciousness as every nerve-ending in his body had screamed with pain. Did this have something to do with the warp—warping?—Bram Forest had mentioned. Hultax the Abarian did not know. But he did know that he was alive, as alive as anyone could be or had a right to be in the Place of the Dead. And he did know, gratefully, that the intense cold of the River of Ice was gone.

He wondered how long he had been unconscious. He blinked his eyes. A balmy, pink-tinted sky. A pink sun, not on the horizon, when indeed the sun might be pink, but overhead. On the horizon—Hultax blinked again and thought he was mad—a second sun, smaller, paler, the ghost of green in color.

The royal barge was in ruins. It had piled up on some rocks. The bier of Jlomec, Prince of Nadia, had been thrown clear. He could see it on the bank, also in ruins. He stood up unsteadily, then waded through the shallow water in which he'd regained consciousness, over to the wreck of the royal barge. The fingers of his right hand were poised inches from the hilt of his whip-sword. Slay Bram Forest and the girl if the wreck hadn't already killed them? He shook his head. Bram Forest knew more about this strange place, this world of the pink sun and the green sun, than he did.

He climbed over the wreckage, and finally came upon the two bodies. He went down on his knees beside them. They were covered with blood. They were broken—broken being the only word that could describe them. They had been crushed, perhaps by falling timber, perhaps by the bier of Jlomec as it hurtled over the side. There probably was not a bone in either of their bodies, at least a major bone, which had not been crushed.

They were dead.

With a craftiness, which surprised even himself, Hultax remembered the dead Bram Forest's words. It was the bracelet with the shining disc which gave Bram Forest the power to appear and disappear at will, as Retoc had, described. Or, as Bram Forest had put it, to journey between the worlds. Carefully, Hultax took the bracelet—it was miraculously intact—from the crushed, broken arm of Bram Forest's corpse. He circled his own arm with it and felt, or imagined he felt, an instantaneous source of power surge through his body. Without looking back at the broken bodies of the man and woman who had found love and, finding it, died in each other's arms, he made his way from the river bank across a pleasant green meadow. Far in the distance he saw a dark blur which looked like a forest. It was many miles away, almost at the limit of vision.

Yet, incredibly, it seemed to rush up at him. It was not merely that Hultax the Abarian walked with a warrior's long stride toward the forest. It was as if the forest rushed toward him. A different world. He remembered Bram Forest's words vaguely. A warped world? Something like that. Naturally, Hultax was afraid. This was the Place of the Dead, wasn't it? But still, Bram Forest's cool if little-understood scientific explanation quieted his fear. Besides, didn't he have the bracelet-disc-amulet? What could happen to him now?

Bylanus the Golden Ape, only two-thousand seven hundred years old, quite young as Golden Apes went, saw the wreck of the barge from a great distance. He extended his vision through warp-space and spotted the tiny figure of a man trudging away from the wreckage. Bylanus squinted, and shifted his buttocks on the saddle. Bylanus was fifteen feet tall and weighed eight-hundred pounds. The steed he rode, about twice the size of an Earth elephant, looked like a blown-up cross between a Tarthian stad and an Earth horse.

Bylanus stared, then sat up very straight in his stirrups. Something gleamed on the man's arm. Bylanus gaped.

It was the bracelet of Portox-saviour.

Bylanus used his will to psychokinesthize the man. The man, still apparently trudging along, sped toward him.

Bylanus climbed down from his stallion and prepared to bow, all fifteen feet and eight hundred pounds of him, before the man.

At first Hultax could think only of fleeing. Abruptly before him stood a monster-stad and a man. No, not a man. A man-like figure pelted with soft, smooth, lustrous, golden fur. The stad—the not-quite-stad—was five times bigger than a stad had a right to be. The man, even as he unexpectedly bent before Hultax, was almost three times Hultax's height. Man? No, not a man. Hultax, rooted with fear to the spot, unable to run, opened his mouth to cry out. But his vocal chords were paralyzed.

This was no man. It was the Golden Ape of legend, the Golden Ape of the Place of the Dead...

"Portox-saviour," said the Golden Ape quite distinctly. Then he pointed a forefinger almost the size of Hultax' forearm at the bracelet Hultax wore.

Hultax took a deep breath and could feel the strength returning to his legs. Like all military officers, he was an opportunist. He had to be, for in battle one had to seize upon opportunity as soon as it appeared, if one were to win at all...

Hultax said, his voice surprisingly steady : "You may rise."

The Ape did so. The stallion pawed the ground, and great clods flew. Hultax was trembling, but the Ape, speaking in Hultax' own language, in the language of all Tarth, said: "Are you really from Portox? It seems like only yesterday he was here although, of course, your people and mine measure time differently."

"I am from Portox," Hultax said. He wished he could keep his knees from trembling.

"Portox-saviour said that one day a man would come, to ask us for help even as Portox helped us in our time of troubles," the Ape proclaimed.

"Yes," Hultax muttered.

"What kind of help do you wish?"

Hultax stared, saying nothing. He did not know what to say. He lacked the imagination to make something up. Somehow, he knew it was terribly important. He knew without knowing how he knew that his life might depend on his answer.

"Well?" the Golden Ape asked gently.

"I...that is..."

The Ape's eyes narrowed as he looked down at Hultax. "You *are* from Portox?"

"Yes, yes. Of course."

"I see you have the bracelet."

"Yes, here is the bracelet."

"And the cloak of Portox?" demanded the Ape. "The cloak Portox foretold you would wear?"

"I—I lost the cloak in my journey," lied Hultax, not knowing about any cloak. There, he thought, that ought to satisfy him.

But the Ape said: "There was no cloak."

"No cloak? No cloak!"

"I made that up, to test you. You're not from Portox."

The stallion pawed the ground and looked up and then down at Hultax, snorting. Hultax, trembling, wished he could melt into the ground.

"Still," Hultax said, shaking, "I am from Portox. You tried to trick me. You…"

"We shall see," the Ape said, still pleasantly. "Come."

The ground rolled, or so it seemed to Hultax. The forest loomed ahead of him, then trees were all around him, then they stood on a rolling plain again.

"Where—did you take me?"

The Ape smiled. He seemed quite human despite his size, despite his fur. The stallion pawed the ground impatiently.

"Behold," said the Ape.

Something on the fringe of the forest screamed. It was an awful sound and it made the hackles stand upright on Hultax's bull-neck. He drew his whip-sword and faced the forest.

"Well, man," chided the Golden Ape, "and do you need a weapon? Portox told us we would know his man because his man, unarmed, would be able to conquer the wild boar of the Kranuian Wood. And you?"

The screaming came again. Terrified, Hultax did not fling his weapon aside. Wild boar? What wild boar…time enough later…to convince the Ape…

The boar emerged. It was almost as big as a man and covered with dirty gray hair. Its tusks were two feet long. The stallion whinnied but remained perfectly still. The Golden Ape waited and watched. The boar charged.

Hultax's right arm blurred and the mobile blade of the whip-sword whizzed through air and struck the boar's meaty shoulder. The boar screamed, and came on.

It was, Hultax realized in despair, only a superficial wound. The boar came on, bleeding, furious. He tried to lunge aside. He yanked at the whip-sword and it came loose, making him lose his balance. The boar reached him, screaming.

Never slackening its pace, the boar gored him, and wheeled about, clods flying, to gore again. Hultax' voice bubbled in his throat. The boar was on him again, its tusks sharp as razors...

Finally it stood clear, nervously eyeing Bylanus and the stallion. Then it turned and, slowly, with great dignity, retreated into the Kranuian Wood, which was its home.

The man, Bylanus saw at a glance, was dead. As an imposter, he had deserved to die. Bylanus quickly dug a shallow grave with a large, sharp-edged stone, and rolled the body in. As he did so he noticed that the bracelet—the bracelet of Portox-saviour, or, more probably, a copy of that bracelet intended to trick him—had been battered, punctured, and broken by the boar. Even if it had been the real bracelet, the amazing steel-silver disc of Portox-saviour, it would now be useless. Sighing, Bylanus buried it with Hultax' body.

Bylanus mounted his steed and galloped toward the river. He could have psychokinesthized himself there, but the day was brilliant and clear, and he was in no great hurry. At last he reached the wreck of the royal barge of Nadia. He did not pause to examine Jlomec's bier, he had seen such funerary devices before.

Something in the wreck itself confused him. There was a man. There was a woman. That fit the ritual—two servants to accompany dead royalty on its way. This was the custom of the Nadians. But the man...

On the man's crushed arm, the arm completely covered with blood, was a mark. It was as if something—say, a band of metal—had protected the arm at one point. For circling the upper arm was a band of skin not bloody like the rest, wide in the shape of a disc, then narrow all around.

The bracelet of Portox-saviour! thought Bylanus. Had this dead man worn it? Had the imposter, now slain by the wild boar, taken it from him?

Oh Portox-saviour, Portox-saviour, how long dead? Am I too late, is it too late for this man, your heir...?

As gently as he could, the huge Bylanus lifted the two bodies and put them in his saddlebags. He faced the Kranuian Wood astride. The stallion held its head up, alert, ready. They psychokinesthized.

And disappeared in a twinkling with Bram Forest and Ylia, both of whom were dead.

CHAPTER SIXTEEN
The Raging Beast

ALTHOUGH once mighty Ofridia of Tarth and certainly the nations of Earth had outstripped Bylanus' world in the physical science, the planet of the pink and green suns was supreme in biology. Thus had it needed Portox' help, a hundred Earth-Tarthian years before, when run-down entropy threatened its very existence. On the other hand, through biology, the science of Bylanus' world had come a long way in the conquest of death and destroyed human tissue. So it was that with some faint ray of confidence Bylanus brought the two broken bodies to the single large city of his park-like planet. There, tenderly, he left them in the care of specialists at the regeneration station, and began his long vigil.

...sensation and movement.

Hardly anything at first. Bram Forest dreamed of dreaming. The motion was gentle, warm, comfortable.

The glow of life and not the cold breath of death...

With it; with the first stirrings of regeneration, came the shadow of pain. But it was far away and almost impalpable, pain understood rather than felt. And slowly the pain departed. There came a time when Bram Forest realized he was not breathing, was, indeed, immersed in liquid.

He floated, helpless, serene, strangely content.

...Until, with the first signs of impatience, strength flooded through his regenerated limbs.

"In every cell of a living creature's body," Orro the bio-technician explained to Bylanus, "there is the potential for complete and perfect regeneration. For, whereas the eye is an organ to see with, in every one of the millions of tiny cells making up the eye is the gene-pattern not merely for the eye but for the rest of the body. Theoretically then, Bylanus, if we are given but a single intact cell of a living—or once-living—organism, we ought to be able to reproduce the organism in its entirety. This is not supernatural. It is not creation of life: we can create nothing. The secret of creation is not ours here at this laboratory. But we have mastered the secret of recreation. Nurtured by the life-giving fluid, their development controlled by their own genes, the two human beings you brought are being made whole again."

Bylanus nodded. Orro the bio-technician was loquacious and spoke quickly, confidently, with mild pedantic enthusiasm. As for Bylanus, he awaited the re-generation of the man who had worn Portox-saviour's bracelet. He looked at the bodies in the vat, hanging upside-down, floating head down, rocking gently in the warm, circulating life-fluid. He waited...

Bram Forest took his first breath. The first thing he said was: "Ylia, Ylia..."

Bylanus met them after the vat had been drained and a door had opened for them. He told them what had happened, including the death of Hultax. Then he added:

"As far as I am concerned, there can be no doubt as to your identity. But the bracelet is lost forever and there will be some who doubt your identity." Abruptly, he seemed to change the subject: "How do you feel?"

"Good as new," Bram Forest said. He was naked. He was tingling with health and well-being, as if he'd awakened from a long, health-giving sleep. He looked at Ylia, her skin glowing, her hair gleaming, her glorious body a shining promise. Then he frowned. Bylanus' words took meaning. "You want me to fight the Boar of the Kranuian Wood, is that it?"

"Yes," Bylanus said.

Bram Forest shrugged. "Coming here was not my idea, although Portox somehow realized it would be so."

"Slay the Kranuian Boar, proving your identity without question, and all the Golden Apes will be yours to command."

"Yes, but did Portox really feel I must wreak upon Abaria and the Abarians the same destruction they brought to Ofridia? If I destroy Retoc the Abarian responsible for what happened a hundred years ago, wouldn't that be enough? I don't need the Golden Apes for that. I can do it myself. I must do it myself."

"Tarth," said Bylanus, "is a world of warring nations. But here on the planet of two suns we live in peace. We are strong but know not the meaning of war. Is that what Portox-saviour wished for your people?"

"Perhaps," Bram Forest said.

"Then," Ylia told him, speaking for the first time, "even if you slay Retoc, his legions will not willingly give up their arms."

Bram Forest nodded slowly. The idea of a Tarth-wide holocaust did not appeal to him, but if all Tarth could be shown the folly of war when its most powerful army went down to defeat before the Golden Apes…

"Thank you," Bram Forest said humbly to the Golden Ape. He had a vision—almost mystical—of a time in the future, perhaps the near future, when all Tarth knew nothing but the ways of peace. "When we return on the River of Ice we want you to accompany us. I'm ready to meet your boar."

Ylia held him. Tears glistened in her eyes. "Bram Forest," she said tremulously. "Now that I've found you, I don't want you to be hurt—ever again."

Bram Forest responded: "Don't worry, Ylia. If Portox hadn't known I'd be more than a match for the boar, he never would have established its conquest as proof of my identity."

"But...but don't you see, you've been re-generated, as Bylanus said. You may not be as strong as you were."

Bram Forest looked at Bylanus, who shrugged. Bylanus lifted them when Bram Forest nodded. The park-like terrain flashed by. A dark forest loomed. The Kranuian Wood...

Close at hand, an animal screamed.

"How do I look, Prokliam?" Volna asked her seneschal.

He bowed before her. "You are lovely, O My Queen."

Volna smiled. She wore the royal purple of Nadia in a gown which fell, clinging as if sentient and voluptuous, to the wonderful curves of her body. "I'm not your Queen yet," she said, laughing.

"A mere formality, My Queen."

"I am Volna, Virgin Princess of Nadia, sister to Bontarc the King."

"Huh!" snorted the old man. "That is your official title. But what do titles matter? When this day ends you will rule all Tarth side by side with Retoc the Abarian."

Yes, Volna thought. With Retoc the Abarian. But how long would *that* alliance last? Would either of them be content to share power with the other? Wouldn't there come a day when she would give the nod to Prokliam and the legions would march against those of Abaria chanting, "All power to Volna! All power to Volna the Beautiful!" The thought of power, power over strong men, over leaders of nations, made her giddy with desire.

All the royal blood of Tarth was gathered in Nadia City now, for the funeral games. She knew Retoc's plan, her spies had confirmed it. Retoc's legions would slay the rulers of the multiple nations and clans of Tarth and one by one, stunned, leaderless, the small nations would flock to the banners of Abaria and Nadia. If, then, Retoc had in mind to betray her and claim all power for himself, her own legions would be rested and ready. And Bontarc? she thought. What of Bontarc, her brother?

As if he could read her thoughts, Prokliam said, "I have arranged the lists for the dueling, which will end the games, majesty. Bontarc, as you know, expects a duel to the first blood with some competent whip-swordsman." Prokliam licked his thin, dry lips. "He will be confronted, instead by a duel to the death with Retoc, the best swordsman of all Tarth. To flee would mean cowardice. The army would then be loyal to you, majesty. To remain and fight would mean only one thing."

"Death," said Volna softly.

She could hear the legions. The legions seemed to chant in her ears: "All power to Volna the Beautiful!"

She thought of the day's funeral games. Games for the memory of Jlomec the Prince, indeed. They were games for her, for Volna. They would be a party celebrating the rise to power of Volna, Virgin Princess of Nadia. But of course neither Nadia nor Bontarc its rightful ruler knew that yet. And when they did, Retoc and his legions would make sure they could do nothing about it.

The Games would be a feast. Volna's feast...

All power to Volna.

The Kranuian Boar came screaming from the forest.

Its small, close-set eyes found Bram at once. If it had seen Bylanus and Ylia, it ignored them. Four hundred pounds of muscle and sinew, it made, stomping and pawing, for Bram.

He side-stepped nimbly, saw the massive head go down, felt one of the wicked tusks brush his thigh with fire. He stumbled and almost fell. If he fell, he would not rise again. The boar would finish him first.

"Bram Forest!" Ylia screamed.

He got up and grasped the tusks. He was dragged along, furrowing the ground. The huge head snorted close to his own. The boar's breath almost made him gag. Then, before the boar could smash him into a tree-trunk, he let go and rolled over and over and quickly stood up.

The boar did not wait for him to regain his breath, but came charging at once. This time Bram Forest waited until the last possible instant before the tusks would impale him. Then he leaped, twisting around in air. It was a prodigious leap and brought a word of exclamation even to Bylanus' lips. He landed on the hard-muscled back of the boar and at once clamped his knees firmly against its sinewy flanks as if he had been trained all his life for this job.

The boar reared and bucked and swung its great body from side to side, trying to dislodge its tormentor. But Bram Forest clung as if all Tarth depended on the out come of this contest—as, perhaps, it did.

The boar ducked its head. Bram Forest fell forward, but his knees locked. The boar rolled over, but moving so swiftly that the eye could hardly follow him, Bram Forest squirmed out from under and was seated astride again when the boar got to its feet.

Then, leaning forward, Bram Forest grasped the two tusks and began to pull the boar's head up and back toward him.

The animal's screaming became squealing. Slowly the head went back, the short, almost non-existent neck strained, the beady eyes darted.

Then there was a loud snapping sound and the boar squealed once and fell over on its side with a broken neck.

Bram Forest, panting, the muscles of his legs quivering, stood clear. Bylanus touched his great golden head to the ground. Ylia ran to Bram Forest and flung her arms about his neck. "I was afraid," she said. "I was so afraid you would be hurt."

Bram Forest kissed her. She clung to him, sobbing his name when their lips parted. Finally Bram Forest disengaged himself and said:

"The poem, Ylia. We've seen an ape, a boar, a stallion. This world is the 'land beyond the stars.' But was the boar also the raging beast?"

Ylia shrugged. Bylanus stood up and told Bram Forest, "The Golden Apes are ready to serve you in any way you wish."

Three worlds, Bram Forest thought. One which Portox had saved from doom, one which had been the haven in which Bram Forest had grown to manhood, and one in which all their destinies soon would be written.

"Then Tarth thanks you," Bram Forest told the Golden Ape Bylanus. "Assemble your fighters. We're going back up the River of Ice."

"To Nadia City?" Ylia asked.

Bram Forest nodded grimly. "To Nadia City—and Retoc."

Bontarc, King of Nadia, asked his royal guest, "You like the Games so far?"

They sat, with Princess Volna, in the box of honor at the Amphitheater of Nadia. "Aye, I like them," Retoc said slowly. "But sire, I would like them much better if they were not to commemorate the passing of your noble brother, the Prince Jlomec."

Bontarc nodded his head in gratitude. "That was well-spoken, Retoc," he said.

Retoc went on: "Have you any idea who killed him so treacherously? Jlomec was not a fighting man."

"None," Bontarc admitted. He missed entirely the smile, which passed between Retoc and Princess Volna.

"Well," Bontarc said after a while, "if you will excuse me, I must go down below to prepare for the dueling. Under the circumstances I'm hardly inclined to participate in the Games, but my people expect it of me."

"Yes, brother," Volna said softly. "They do. Oh, they do."

And Bontarc went. Retoc looked at Volna. "I'd best get ready myself," he said. Volna nodded her lovely head.

A blood-lusting animal cry welled up from a hundred thousand throats as the gladiators of Nadia marched out across the sands of the amphitheater to do battle with the fierce snow-sloths of the Plains of Ice.

While several jeks from the Gates of Ice, Retoc's legions waited...

"Wait here," Bram Forest told Bylanus, who had led them safely, along with the vanguard of the Golden Apes, back up the River of Ice.

"What will you do, Bram Forest?"

"According to Ylia, we can trust Bontarc of Nadia. He's a fighting man, but he craves peace for all Tarth."

"I'm sure of it," Ylia said. "Bontarc didn't send us to the Place of the Dead. Princess Volna did. And long ago, according to the stories the Wayfarers of Ofrid tell, Bontarc and your mother, Queen Evalla, were allies striving to establish universal peace throughout Tarth. Besides, despite his civility and fairness, Bontarc loses no love on Retoc of Abaria."

"And if you need us?" Bylanus asked.

"We'll get a signal through to you," Bram Forest said. With Ylia he climbed into a skiff and poled it out into the river.

Now the riverbanks were deserted, except for the solitary stiltbirds, tall as men, wading out into the frigid water, their low-pitched calls all but swallowed by the sound the cold wind made rustling through the river rushes.

After a while the skiff came to a bend in the river. It was the last turn before the Gates of Ice—and Nadia City. Here the wind blew more strongly, and there was a section of rushes, which had been cleared, cut probably by an Ice Fields nomad who had used the tall rushes as fuel.

"Look!" Ylia cried suddenly, startled.

Through the gap in the rushes, at a distance of two or three jeks across the flat plain from the river, Bram Forest saw an armed encampment. There were tents with flying standards, tethered stads, pyramids of stacked spears like hayricks, and pacing sentries.

"What can it mean?" Ylia asked. "Those standards are Abarian."

"Retoc," Bram Forest said. He lifted the pole and felt the mud of the river-bottom cling to it before it came clear. He allowed the skiff to drift toward the bank. "Retoc's planning treachery. We'll have to go back and alert the Golden Apes. Bylanus and his Apes can destroy Retoc's legions before they even march on Nadia City."

"But we can't go back, Bram. If Retoc's army is here, ready, then what's happening in Nadia City? Who can say what Retoc is doing? You'll have to go ahead and stop him—or at least delay him. I'll go back for Bylanus."

Bram Forest shook his head. "I can't let you go alone, Ylia. Not with the Abarian legions so close."

"But I must, don't you see?"

Bram Forest frowned. There did not seem any other way, but he was reluctant. "I love you, Ylia. I couldn't let—"

"What happens in Nadia City today is more important

than our love, Bram Forest! What would our love mean if Retoc the Abarian ruled all Tarth?"

"Then you take the skiff," Bram Forest said finally. "I can make my way to the city along the bank."

"No. The army is still encamped. They won't do anything for some time yet. See? All their tents are still standing."

That was true enough. "Besides," Ylia went on, "we don't know what Retoc is planning in the city. You can reach it faster by skiff. I'll go back for Bylanus on foot."

The logic of what Ylia said could not be refuted. With sinking heart Bram Forest helped her from the skiff. He kissed her quickly. "I love you, Ylia," he said.

"And I love you, Bram Forest."

"Be careful. Keep hidden in the rushes. Tell Bylanus to use his judgment in attacking or waiting for Retoc's legions to make the first move."

Ylia's pretty head nodded. Then she ducked into the rushes and was gone. Bram Forest looked after her until the rustling in the rushes stopped, then he poled the skiff once more out into the center of the river and sped swiftly toward the Gates of Ice.

No one stopped him. No guards were posted. He beached the skiff and sprinted through the gates and through the city and up its biggest hill toward the amphitheater. Then, only a jek's distance away, he heard the crowd at the funeral games. They roared suddenly in a frenzy of excitement and another part of Portox's poem slipped into place. The crowd watching the games in Nadia City was the raging beast, blood-lusting, expectant, animal-savage, whipped into a fever of goggle-eyed enthusiasm and ready to move, *en-masse*, in whatever direction a strong leader might push them.

A strong leader...

Retoc? Or Bram Forest? Which one?

Pirum the Abarian shifted his weight uncomfortably, leaning down on the haft of his spear. The whole idea of posting pickets along the bank of the river seemed unnecessary to him. They could not actually see the river through the rushes, and they dared not go closer for fear of being spotted by whatever traffic moved on the icy waters. Then what was the point of them standing here, half frozen with the cold, waiting for an assailant who would never come?

And while he was thinking thus, the girl virtually walked into Pirum's arms. At first he heard a faint rustling in the rushes and, before he could investigate, the tallest of the dry plants had parted and a lovely bronze-skinned girl appeared. She turned to run, but Pirum caught her in his muscular arms and held her despite her struggles.

She bit his arm and, with an oath, he caught her hair and twisted her head back. "Who are you?" he said. "Who are you, eh?"

The girl glowered at him.

Pirum dragged her along. She continued to struggle. Shaking his head, he hit her on the jaw with his fist and caught her before she could fall. Then, swinging her up over his broad shoulder, he stalked through the rushes toward Nadia City.

CHAPTER SEVENTEEN
The Prison Without Bars

NO ONE tried to stop Bram Forest until he reached the very gates of the amphitheater. But there a guard with drawn whip-sword barred the way and demanded: "You don't look Nadian to me. What delegation are you with, man?"

Bram Forest had no time to parry words with words. He tried to push his way past the guard who, too surprised to thrust with his weapon, used his free hand to grab Bram Forest by the shoulder and spin him around. Bram Forest drove his left fist into the guard's belly and heard the whoosh of air escaping from his lungs.

That was the last thing he heard for some time. A second guard crept up quietly behind him and struck expertly with the hilt of his whip-sword just behind the left ear. Bram Forest fell as if the ground dropped out from under him.

"By all the fiery gods of Tarth, will you look at that!" the first guard exclaimed.

The second guard could only gawk, not comprehending.

The unconscious man was growing tenuous.

The first guard in confused alarm, lashed down with the whip-sword. But its point passed through Bram Forest's now transparent body without meeting any resistance.

"Right through him! Right through him!" cried the guard.

And, by the time he said it, and coiled his sword again, Bram Forest had vanished.

When an urgent message had come for Retoc, the Princess Volna, alone in the royal box, had decided to investigate the matter herself. She had to hurry, though. In not many minutes, Retoc and Bontarc would find themselves face to face on the sands of the amphitheater. Wouldn't Bontarc be surprised! Too proud to flee, not swordsman enough to match the mighty Retoc...

"Yes, yes, what is it?" she snapped irritably when she entered the dungeon-like ready-room below the amphitheater sands. She was in a hurry to return to her box, less she miss the duel between Bontarc and Retoc. Alone in the ready-room was a soldier in the uniform of Abaria.

"Begging your pardon, ma'am," said the soldier. "My message is for Retoc of Abaria."

"And I tell you Retoc of Abaria is not here to receive it." Volna clapped her hands and two of her own guards appeared. "I am the Princess Volna. Well?"

Pirum looked at her, at the armed guards flanking her on either side, at the door through which she had entered, at the ready-room's second door. "Very well," he said at last, and opened the second door, beckoning.

Volna went to the doorway and looked. She gasped involuntarily, hardly able to believe her eyes. There on the stone floor of a smaller ready-room, only now regaining consciousness, was the Virgin Wayfarer of Ofrid, she who had seen Retoc slay Jlomec, she who had been sent by Volna herself to sure death on the Journey of No Return. Terror gripped her.

"What does this mean?" Volna cried. "Where did you find her? Where, man? Speak!"

"On the river, ladyship."

"On the river? Returning from the Place of the Dead?"

"No, ladyship. Heading toward the Place of the Dead."

Volna went to the girl and stood over her. "You! What's your name?"

"Ylia," the girl said.

"What were you trying to do, Ylia?"

The girl said nothing.

Volna called to Pirum, who came at once. "Hit her," Volna said.

Grasping Ylia by her hair, Pirum struck her face with his open hand. Her head snapped back. The mark of his fingers was on her face. She said nothing.

"Hit her again," Volna said.

Pirum struck Ylia a second time. The girl whimpered, but held her tongue. "Where is your friend, that giant of a man?" Volna asked.

Again Pirum hit Ylia when she would say nothing. Finally Volna shrugged. "She'll talk, given enough of that. What's *your* name, man?"

"Pirum, ladyship."

"Very well, Pirum. My guards and I are returning to our seats. There is a duel I wouldn't want to miss. All Tarth will reap its consequences. Meanwhile, stay with this girl and do what you must do to make her talk. It might be important."

Pirum bowed. "Yes, ladyship," he said, and watched the others depart. Then, when they were alone, Ylia surprised him by flying at him, nails bared, like a wildcat. He fought off her attack and struck her a savage openhanded blow, and she fell back. At least this, Pirum thought advancing on her, might be an interesting assignment.

"...hit by that cab, mac."

"You all right?"

"He's getting up, ain't he?"

"Jeez, I swear," the sweating taxi driver said to the crowd which had gathered about the prostrate man, "he popped up outa nowhere. One second I'm driving along, looking for a fare, the next, he's standing right in front of me. I almost pushed the brake through the floor, honest, but—"

"Ylia," the stricken man said.

"Hey now, take it easy."

"What he say, anyhow?"

"... be going to a costume ball or something. Lookit that outfit he's wearing, willya? What's he supposed to be, a man from Mars or something? I read in the papers where Mars was pretty close a while back. My kid thinks there are..."

"Aw, shudap about your kid."

"Need any help, mister?"

"No. No, thank you. I'm all right."

"...got a nasty crack on his head, is all. See? See the blood?"

"He's getting up."

"...a cop. When you don't want 'em, they're around. Now you need them, where in heck are they, that's what I wanna know."

"The bracelet!" the stricken man said in sudden alarm. He stared at his own right arm in confusion, then his left. His arms were bare.

"You wasn't wearing no bracelet, mac," someone said.

"No bracelet," he said. "No bracelet." His eyes looked vague, confused.

After a while a policeman came and took in the situation at a glance. "All right, all right," he bawled. "Step back and givemair, givemair, will you?"

The crowd dispersed slowly, and the policeman talked for a while with the taxidriver, then with the stricken man.

"My name?" the stricken man said in answer to a question. "Bram Forest. Yes, Bram Forest. But I don't have the bracelet. The bracelet is gone, forever. Without the bracelet I can't..." his voice trailed off.

"He drunk?" the policeman asked the cab driver.

"Search me."

" 'A prison without bars,' " the man recited. "Earth is my prison, forever. Ylia. Ylia!"

The driver made a circular motion with his forefinger, in the general vicinity of his temple.

"You both better come down the station house with me," the policeman said.

"Aw, officer, I'll lose some fares."

"Anyhow. The guy talks batty, but he don't look drunk. We got to figure this here out."

"Ylia," the man said, almost as if the sound were a name and he was crying out to the owner of that name across an unthinkable abyss.

Bontarc, King of Nadia, felt as good as could be expected under the circumstances. Now that the first shock of bereavement had passed, he knew no mourning would bring back his dead brother Jlomec. And the sun of Tarth was hot on the amphitheater sands as Bontarc stood awaiting his as yet unknown adversary. He flexed and uncoiled his whip-sword, smiling in expectancy. He was a competent swordsman, among the dozen or so best in Nadia. The duel-to-first-blood would be just what he needed. Win or lose, he'd feel a lot better afterwards. And meanwhile, he was a king, wasn't he? The adulation of the crowd swept down all around him, lifting his spirits. The corpse of Prince Jlomec, treacherously slain, seemed very far away—as, indeed, it was...

A roar of expectancy went up from a hundred thousand throats as Bontarc's adversary appeared at the other end of the arena. The sun was dazzling. At first Bontarc saw the swordsman only as a dot across the gleaming sands. But now the roar of expectancy had turned to a groan of dismay, which was followed by a silence, as of death, then an eager whispered buzzing. Why should this be? Why...

The figure came closer on the burning sands. Bontarc squinted. Was it possible? He felt a tremor go through his body.

It was Retoc of Abaria!

"To the death, Bontarc," Retoc said softly, savagely, as they approached.

Bontarc shook his head imperceptibly. He was no coward, but knew he was no match for Retoc and didn't see why he should lay down his life on the amphitheater sands. "I'll not fight you to the death, Retoc of Abaria," he said.

Retoc shrugged as if it weren't very important. "Well," he said slowly, "if you don't want to kill the slayer of your brother..."

Bontarc charged.

Laughing, Retoc was ready for him.

"...Please...please...you're just wasting your time. I...won't...tell you."

"No?" Pirum said, panting. He saw the girl through a haze of anger, frustration, and desire. She was naked, her lips were bloody, but her eyes still flashed defiance. Pirum, like most Abarians, was something of a sadist.

"Oh, you'll talk," he said. "You'll talk."

"...never..."

He dug his strong finger cruelly into her tender body.

"Bram Forest..." she cried.

The policeman behind the desk was saying things. Bram Forest heard the droning voice, but not the words. Ylia, he thought. Ylia. A moment before, he actually believed he heard her cry out to him in pain. But that couldn't be. Besides, what could he do about it? He was trapped forever on Earth, without the bracelet, which could send him, almost on the wings of thought, back to Tarth, to Ylia, to his destiny.

I love you, girl of Tarth, he thought. *I love you, Ylia, more than words and more than worlds.*

Something whisperingly cold plucked at him, and for an instant his heart was stilled.

Ylia!

Could his love for the girl of Tarth draw him across the unthinkable abyss?

"...immodestly attired and..." the desk sergeant was saying.

Ylia, Ylia, call me! Draw me to you, girl of Tarth.

...bramforesthelp...

Ylia! I hear you! I hear you!

"What the heck's he doing? Praying?" the patrolman asked.

For Bram Forest was staring devoutly at nothing, staring at the air in front of his face there in the mundane precinct room as if it held a radiant vision.

Suddenly the desk sergeant's jaw dropped open. The patrolman said: "Hey; wait a mo..."

Bram Forest was becoming tenuous, vanishing.

Insubstantial, transparent, the image of Bram Forest soared past the encampment of the Golden Apes. "Bylanus!" he called, and his voice was not insubstantial. Bylanus came at once.

"If the Abarian legions move, attack them, Bylanus."

"As you will, Bram Forest. But you..."

"Don't worry about me. I can control it, I can control it."

Bylanus passed an enormous hand through Bram Forest's body.

"I'll materialize, when I find Ylia. She draws me..." Already the vision was fading.

"Farewell, Bram Forest."

Farewell.

Was it merely the sound of the wind along the banks of the River of Ice? Bylanus wondered.

Something struck Pirum's shoulder. The girl crouched, sobbing, at his feet. Pirum whirled.

His face went white when he saw the man. He swung his fist desperately, and the man blocked it without effort. His arm was caught, as in a vise. He screamed. Something snapped in his arm. Something streaked at his face...

He took the blow from Bram Forest's fist under the point of the jaw. His head snapped back against the dungeon wall and memory and desire and lust and life oozed out through his smashed skull.

"Ylia!"

"You came, Bram Forest."

"I'll never leave you again."

"Yes, now, in the amphitheater. I think..."

Overhead, the crowd roared. Bram Forest listened for a fraction of a second, and raced for the stairs.

When word of the duel between Bontarc and Retoc came by courier to Laugrim, second in command of the Abarian army under the missing Hultax, Laugrim decided it was time to attack. He gave the signal for his army to march on the city, and the signal was passed from signal-fire to signal-fire in the huge encampment. In a very short time, the army's vanguard began to march. *There's no force on all Tarth strong enough to stop us now*, Laugrim thought exultantly. *This day, Retoc would rule Tarth.*

He was right. There was no Tarthian army strong enough to stop them. But the Army of the Golden Apes which, after Bram Forest's warning, had deployed itself at the very gates of Nadia City so the people in the amphitheater might witness the battle, was not of Tarth...

"Well, Bontarc," cried Retoc, "can't you do better than that? Surely a king..."

For many minutes now Retoc, the finest swordsman on Tarth, had been toying with his adversary. He could have killed Bontarc a dozen times over, but he waited, driving the Nadian ruler back, playing with him, making him do incredible gymnastics in order to survive, three times returning his whip-sword to him when it had been torn from the Nadian's hands.

All Nadia—and all the rulers of Tarth—watched spellbound. It seemed to them that the Nadian ruler had gone into the contest willingly. They made no move, and under the ethics that governed their world, would make no move, to stop the uneven contest.

Retoc's blurring swordpoint whipped and flashed, drawing blood from a dozen superficial wounds. The smile never left Retoc's face. Desperately, knowing his life was forfeit whenever Retoc chose, Bontarc parried the whiplashing blade.

Bram Forest emerged into the dazzling sunlight of the arena floor. Squinting, he saw the figures across the sand.

The men before him were Bontarc of Nadia and Retoc, slayer of his mother, destroyer of Ofridia.

Retoc saw him first, and cried out exultantly. His wrist blurred, his whip-sword flashed, the point singing, and Bontarc's sword flew from his fingers. "You!" Retoc cried.

The sword-point had slashed an artery on Bontarc's wrist. The blood spurted out and Bontarc stood there, dazed, holding the wound shut with his left hand.

"Are you all right, sire?" Bram Forest asked.

"I can manage until a doctor binds—"

Bram Forest picked up the Nadian ruler's whip-sword and faced his enemy, sword to sword, at last.

Retoc looked at him, and laughed. "I almost killed you

once," he said. His hand barely seemed to move, but the point of his blade, whipping, flashing, was everywhere. Bram Forest parried desperately. "I'll finish the job now," Retoc vowed.

Then Bram Forest did an unexpected thing. He used the whip-sword not as a sword: he couldn't hope to match Retoc's skill as a swordsman. He used it as a whip is used, his great arm slicing back and forth through air, up over his head and down, the long length of the uncoiled blading whipping and darting like something alive across the sands.

Retoc retreated two steps, and lunged with what he hoped would be a deathblow.

Prokliam the seneschal was trembling so much he could hardly stand. Just outside the amphitheater, in the very shadow of the amphitheater wall, the great Golden Apes of legend had materialized. There were thousands of them, and they were three times the size of men, and methodically and with great ease, they were destroying the Abarian army before it could enter the amphitheater.

Without the Abarian army, Volna and Retoc would never subjugate Nadia, never rule Tarth. But Prokliam the seneschal had committed himself to their cause. Now only death awaited him.

Or, had he committed himself? Couldn't he change sides before it was too late? Couldn't he slay Volna, here in the royal box, for all to see? Couldn't he become a hero of the people? He was confused. He wished he could think clearly, but he was more frightened than he had ever been in his life. There was something wrong with his logic. Something… Well, no matter. Slay Volna first, call her traitor, and then worry about his logic—

He turned away from the wall and marched down the flights of stairs between the citizens of Nadia, flanked in two wildly shouting mobs on either side of the aisle, and plunged a knife into Volna's back, killing her instantly.

The people roared, and rose up. Like a tide they swept to-ward Prokliam, the seneschal who had wanted to be prime minister.

"No, no!" he cried. "No, please. You don't understand...I see it now...what was wrong with my thinking...you don't know yet...you don't know...to you she was still the Princess Volna, loyal, true...you don't understand, please."

The wave rolled over Prokliam the seneschal, leaving him battered and bloody and dead in its wake.

The strong, whipping motion of Bram Forest's arm made a wall of steel of his whip-sword. Try as he might, with all the skill at his command, Retoc could not dent that wall. But, he thought, there was another way. Slowly, desperately, he maneuvered Bram Forest back toward Bontarc, who was sitting in the sand and using all his remaining energy to hold the life blood in his veins, his fingers clamped, vise-like, about his own arm.

Bram Forest's arm blurred up, down, to either side. He wove a web of death. It was brawn against skill, he knew—and the strength of his arm might win! Retoc was sweating. Retoc was not the cool swordsman he had been moments before. Desperately, Retoc sought an opening, and found none. True, his superior footwork was forcing Bram Forest back across the sand, but what did that matter? Last time they dueled he had made the mistake of meeting Retoc on his own grounds as greatest swordsman of Tarth. This time...

His legs caught against something. He fell heavily.

Retoc's sword-point flashed down.

Bram Forest rolled over, stood up with sand blinding his eyes. For precious moments he could see nothing but could only spin with the whip-sword, slashing air in all directions, hoping Retoc couldn't strike through the wall of steel.

Then, slowly, vision returned to his stinging eyes. Bontarc lay stretched out on the sand now, unconscious, the blood pumping from his severed artery. If he bled like that for more than a few moments, he would die. If he died, and if Nadia rose in its wrath against Abaria, then all that Bram Forest had dreamed of, not revenge against Abaria for a wrong done, but eternal peace on Tarth, would be lost...

He took the offensive, weaving his wall of steel toward Retoc. The Abarian thrust his own sword, and withdrew it, and parried, and lunged and thrust again. The wall of steel, which was Bram Forest's singing blade advanced relentlessly.

Round and round his head, Bram Forest whirled the whip-sword. Retoc could—just—block the motion, the death-laden circle, with his own blade. He became accustomed to it. He used all his effort, all his skill to block it.

Then, abruptly, Bram Forest raised his swordarm and brought it down from high over his head.

Retoc screamed.

And died screaming, his head and torso split from crown to navel.

Bram Forest rushed to Bontarc, stretched out on the sand, and with his own hand stemmed the bleeding.

Bylanus the Golden Ape said: "All Tarth is yours to command if you wish it, Bram Forest."

"No, Bylanus. Take your people back to your world and live in peace. We of Tarth thank you."

Bylanus smiled. "I thought you would say that."

"Portox was a great scientist," Bram Forest said. "But he thought too much of revenge. The ancient wrong is righted.

"Then you'll spare Abaria?" gasped the delegate of the assembled Tarthian nobles, who had come to the meeting called by Bylanus that night.

"My fight was with Retoc and the Abarian army. Retoc is dead, the army decimated and disbanded. My fight with Abaria is over."

"Then what will you do?"

Bram Forest took Ylia's hand. "I'd like to see a great nation rise again on the Plains of Ofrid."

Bontarc, his arm bandaged, said: "My people will help you build. And, with your wayfarers as a nucleus, maid Ylia…"

"It will be a small nation at first," Ylia said.

"It will grow, so long as Tarth knows peace," Bontarc told her.

"Tarth will know nothing but peace from now on," Bram Forest promised.

It was a promise, which he knew all of them would keep.

THE END

If you've enjoyed this book, you will not want to miss these terrific titles...

If you've enjoyed this book, you will not want to miss these terrific titles...

ARMCHAIR SCI-FI & HORROR DOUBLE NOVELS, $12.95 each

ARMCHAIR SCIENCE FICTION CLASSICS, $12.95 each

ARMCHAIR SCI-FI & HORROR GEMS SERIES, $12.95 each

If you've enjoyed this book, you will not want to miss these terrific titles…

ARMCHAIR SCI-FI & HORROR DOUBLE NOVELS, $12.95 each

D-21   **EMPIRE OF EVIL** by Robert Arnette
       THE SIGN OF THE TIGER by Alan E. Nourse & J. A. Meyer

D-22   **OPERATION SQUARE PEG** by Frank Belknap Long
       ENCHANTRESS OF VENUS by Leigh Brackett

D-23   **THE LIFE WATCH** by Lester del Rey
       CREATURES OF THE ABYSS by Murray Leinster

D-24   **LEGION OF LAZARUS** by Edmond Hamilton
       STAR HUNTER by Andre Norton

D-25   **EMPIRE OF WOMEN** by John Fletcher
       ONE OF OUR CITIES IS MISSING by Irving Cox

D-26   **THE WRONG SIDE OF PARADISE** by Raymond F. Jones
       THE INVOLUNTARY IMMORTALS by Rog Phillips

D-27   **EARTH QUARTER** by Damon Knight
       ENVOY TO NEW WORLDS by Keith Laumer

D-28   **SLAVES TO THE METAL HORDE** by Milton Lesser
       HUNTERS OUT OF TIME by Joseph E. Kelleam

D-29   **RX JUPITER SAVE US** by Ward Moore
       BEWARE THE USURPERS by Geoff St. Reynard

D-30   **SECRET OF THE SERPENT** by Don Wilcox
       CRUSADE ACROSS THE VOID by Dwight V. Swain

ARMCHAIR SCIENCE FICTION CLASSICS, $12.95 each

C-7   **THE SHAVER MYSTERY, Book One**
       by Richard S. Shaver

C-8   **THE SHAVER MYSTERY, Book Two**
       by Richard S. Shaver

C-9   **MURDER IN SPACE** by David V. Reed
       by David V. Reed

ARMCHAIR MASTERS OF SCIENCE FICTION SERIES, $16.95 each

M-3   **MASTERS OF SCIENCE FICTION, Vol. Three**
       Robert Sheckley, "The Perfect Woman" and other tales

M-4   **MASTERS OF SCIENCE FICTION, Vol. Four**
       Mack Reynolds, "Stowaway" and other tales

If you've enjoyed this book, you will not want to miss these terrific titles…